M

by Jane Kohle

Twisterella Books
London

author's thanks

Obviously this is written entirely from my point of view. We all coped differently with our situation and both Jordan's Dad Kurt, and myself, did the best we could for her. Mentally, I could only focus on what Jordan was going through, trying to cope with both that and my own emotions. I really didn't have the energy to wonder how everyone else was feeling, not because I didn't care, but because it took all I had just to get through each day. I think that everyone understood this, and hopefully they will realise that they haven't been left out of the diary for any reason other than that I may have forgotten to mention them on a particular day.

Special love and thanks for their continuous support to all Jordan's grandparents.
Tricia, John, Dru, Pam and Jim. To Jordan's uncles and aunts, Jamie, Joanne, Stuart and Lisa.
To the parents and special children we met at G.O.S.H., especially Louise, Leon, Lene, Corinne, Sonny, Josh and Rowan, who is no longer with us but will never be forgotten.
All the staff at G.O.S.H. for trying so hard to help Jordan and for keeping her comfortable when she could no longer be helped to recover.
To Sharon Thornhill and family for all their help and care.
To all the following friends and family who phoned,

visited, sent cards, presents or flowers during our stay: Debbie, Stewart, Chloe and Josh, Jo Kellam, Marie, Derek and Steven, Sally and Alex, Jacquie, Keith, Jo and Clive, Cliff, Charlton and Tim. All at Sheredes Playgroup. Brian and Ann Sullivan, Ruth and Dave, Rosina and Kathryn, Danuta, Jayne, Ken and boys, Carrie and Mike, Roy and Marie, Lid and Bernice, Elizabeth, Albert and Mary, Bob, Elsie and Maura, Pauline, Chris and Cheryl. Pat and family, Aunt Liz, George and Lyn, Rita and Eric, Emma, Jerry, Barbara, Tony and family, Hermine and Jeremy, Pauline and Paul, Albie, Clare, Max and Amy, Kelly, Jon, Lin, Mark and Simone, Barbara A, Francesca and Vic, Judith and Paul, Mark Davis, Margaret, Michael and family, John and June, and Ann, Sonia, Frosa, Leeroy, Bekky and Andy, Carol and all at Ware, Andrea, Jeanette and Anita, Jacky F and family, John T, Lesley and Ray, Andy and Jan, Matt and family.

Thanks to all.

For Jordan...

introduction

I have written this diary primarily for myself and for my daughter Jordan. I did this so that she would know when her first tooth came, her first words, her first steps, everything. I planned to give her the diaries when she was 18 - something unusual to keep and look back on. Now I open its pages to you in the hope that by reading it you may, in some way, be left richer for our story being told.

If you are lucky enough to have the health of your children, then hopefully this book will remind you of just how special a gift they are, something that is often forgotten during the difficult times that growing up brings.

If you, like me, are living through the heartache of nursing or losing a sick child, then hopefully these pages will remind you that you are not alone, no matter how isolated you feel.

I kept up the diary in hospital and this is what you will read. Sixteen weeks worth, just as I wrote it. Some of it is clear, some of it is not, depending on my state of mind at the time.

But what follows is not just a diary. It is the story of how I coped during my daughter's illness and how I found the strength to survive without her at a time when it seemed impossible and worthless to do so. I hope that by the time you turn the final page you too can find the comfort and the strength to make it through.

I was never a particularly maternal person. I liked children but wasn't anxious to have my own. However, when I phoned the Doctor to confirm the results of my pregnancy test, I was thrilled, I couldn't stop smiling. I didn't want to tell anyone until I was about three months, because I knew this was the time when things could go wrong. After that, there was no stopping me.

I was so proud of my bump. I had no morning sickness and few of the usual things related to pregnancy. I did stop eating chicken kiev and started drinking lots of lemonade. I also ate lots of Mars bars, something I had never done before or since.

My due date was given as June 19th, but it never sounded right to me, I thought it would be earlier. True enough, at 11pm on June 15th, I went into labour, very strange feelings in my stomach every ten minutes, which after a while became obvious contractions! I tried to keep calm and busy and upright, as this was the most comfortable. I tried a relaxing bath but I didn't like it. I tried to lie down but I didn't like that either. So I tidied up and checked my bag a few times. That night I couldn't sleep, so at about 7am off we went to the hospital. The contractions were now more fierce and closer together. As I got out of the car, I had one and thought I'd never get across the car park. I then had another in the elevator. Fortunately there was a Nurse with us by now who took me to the labour wards.

Once there, I had monitors put all over my stomach and we were left to listen to the bleeps and blips for a while. I was then taken into the labour room and had my waters broken for me. The contractions came on faster and harder. I only had gas and air. I had wanted as natural a birth as possible, so by the time my back started to hurt it was too late for any other drugs.

There was a bit of a struggle at the final push because I was so tired, but, at 3.08pm on Sunday 16th June, Jordan Marie Kohle-Stephens arrived, weighing 6lb 9oz. Her arrival on Father's Day was the best present Kurt or her two Grandad's could ever have wished for! Kurt said "We've got a smurf!" She was blue and slippery but perfect. They laid her on my stomach for a minute or so before cleaning her up. I had been convinced I would have a boy, so I was surprised, but in no way disappointed.

From the moment Jordan lay on my stomach and I put my hand on her, I was in love. I was over-whelmed and could hardly speak. I couldn't believe that I had given birth to this beautiful baby. Her nails were long and looked freshly manicured and her damp hair (what there was of it) lay in wiggles. I knew it would be curly.

The midwife commented on what a perfectly shaped head Jordan had. That comment still haunts me today...

the beginning

Jordan was beautiful and she was perfect. She never cried. She looked too worldly wise for one so young and she had a calmness and serenity about her that everyone noticed.

I couldn't leave my baby alone, I held her as much as possible. I didn't like other people holding her, I wanted her all to myself. I was told by older, wiser people that I would make her clingy and I'd never be able to leave her, that she'd always want cuddles. I smiled and nodded and ignored them. I loved cuddling her even when she was asleep. I loved to look at her lovely face and kiss her.

She never slept for any great length of time, but I didn't mind being tired. When she was awake, I would lay her on my lap, her head on my knees and feet on my stomach and talk to her. I told her all about myself and her family, about all the things we would do together when she was a big girl, and that her Dad would have to check out all her boyfriends because none of them would ever be good enough for her.

I told Jordan that I didn't mind whatever she did when she was older as long as she was happy and a nice person.

I used to ask her "Are you gorgeous?" and she would smile at me. She loved laying on Kurt's chest and going to sleep. She was the light of our lives and brought more happiness than I could ever have imagined. I was completely besotted.

From the day that she arrived I started to have strange dreams. I would be standing at the window talking to Jordan about what was going on outside and she would slowly leave my arms and float off, out of the window and up towards the sky. We were both calm and she'd be smiling.

When I woke up I would put my hand on her to make sure she was breathing - there was a lot of talk about cot deaths at this time and I was terrified.

I assumed these dreams were normal for a new Mum, afraid to lose her new baby. Now I'm not so sure.

Jordan was a wonderful baby, no trouble at all. Her eating and sleeping habits were a bit erratic but I thought to myself that no two babies are the same, that she was a little person with her own personality and her body would sort itself out in its own time.

She was happy and content and very alert, watching and listening constantly. The first time I took Jordan out in her pram by myself I was so nervous of every lump and bump on the path, of every sudden noise, so much so that when she made some little noises I ran nearly all the way home, happy just to get her back indoors again.

Six weeks after Jordan arrived, my friend Debbie gave birth to Chloe. They lived in a flat downstairs so we all spent a lot of time together. The two girls would lie on a play-mat together, just chuckling and playing.

Jordan's cousin Hollie was born soon after the other two. The three of them were so different, but very loving towards each other, one minute cuddling, the next bashing each other.

Most babies have a blanket or toy that they drag around with them - Jordan liked labels. If she found a label on a blanket or teddy bear, she would roll it between her fingers and thumb, fascinated.

Debbie and I bought a second hand double buggy so that we could take the girls out together. It was really handy, especially if one of us had a Doctor 's appointment or something, it was easier to keep them entertained together. Hollie would also be out in it with Jordan if I was baby-sitting for her Mum. It was one of our brighter ideas and we actually made a couple of pounds when we sold it. When she was in her pram, Jordan was fascinated by trees and as she got bigger she loved going to the park, on the swings, feeding the ducks, just being outside looking at the trees and flowers.

By seven months Jordan was saying "mumum" and "dada". I loved the way she spoke. For bottle she would say "bopple". I taught her to say "please" using grapes, she loved fruit. I'd offer a grape and she'd say "Yes, please" with a little nod of her head. I fed Jordan myself up to nine months, after which her hard gums and sharp edged new teeth became too much for me.

Jordan and Hollie had similar habits. They would sit together holding their bedtime bottles with one hand whilst playing with their hair with the other, which was always a sign of tiredness. If Jordan was sleeping with me, my hair also got played with, twisted and pulled until it hurt, but she was asleep and didn't know she was doing it.

Chloe and Jordan loved going to our local outdoor swimming pool. There was a big field next to it, where we had picnics and played in between swimming. Sometimes they might fall asleep for a while and Debbie and I could sunbathe and relax. We also had a paddling pool which we put in the garden of the flats where we lived. We had picnics there too - we would try anything to make the girls' days interesting, because living in flats and not having our own garden wasn't ideal for two lively toddlers.

Jordan and Chloe joined a mother and toddler group together. They thoroughly enjoyed it, playing with different toys and children and singing songs which we had to sing at home as well. As they grew bigger they got into all sorts of mischief together. They liked nothing better than sneaking into the bedroom and opening drawers, sorting out my underwear, putting on shoes and boots and generally making a mess.

All children seem to like the phone and Jordan loved to hold conversations even when she couldn't speak properly. She would say "Hawo" for hello and nod her head, pull faces and use her hands while chatting. I wondered if that's what I did and if she was copying me.

Jordan's hands were tiny and delicate. She loved books and would turn the pages very carefully. She learned very quickly and would tell me what was coming next in a story. She picked up the alphabet and numbers really well and later on Kurt even taught her a couple of words in French.

If she wanted a better look at something I had or was doing she would say "Just have a look mummy."

Mealtimes were funny, her appetite was always strange, but I tried not to make to much fuss about how little she ate. I didn't want to battle over food in case it put her off. Sometimes she'd pick up bits of food, drop them over the edge of her high-chair and say "All gone" with a satisfied grin on her face. I tried to keep her diet as healthy as possible and luckily she liked fruit and vegetables. Her first strawberries got everywhere, her face, hair and clothes - she thoroughly enjoyed them. When she did start to eat chocolates and sweets, she never ate many.

By Jordan's first birthday she was walking around the furniture continually, occasionally letting go for a couple of seconds. Sometimes she clapped her hands - she knew it was clever.

The night before her first birthday I put balloons up all round the living room. In the morning her face was a picture! Lots of people came around and she got loads of presents, especially clothes. Even at this young age, Jordan loved clothes.

On the 4th July, Jordan walked all day long for the first time. Her own Independence Day! I took photos of her - she was so pleased with herself, laughing, her hands twitching with excitement, going from room to room.

After Jordan started walking I took her to buy some shoes because she wanted to walk outside in the street. I had her feet measured - she was only $2^{1/2}$! They had no shoes small enough, so we had to go back a few weeks later when her feet had spread out a bit from taking her weight. Her first pair were a size 3 and she loved them. She seemed so grown up running around in them.

She loved music and dancing, she had a little side to side wiggle, and a front to back movement with her head 'banging' - it was so funny. Chloe, Jordan and I used to have disco mornings if I was baby-sitting for Debbie, where we'd put tapes or videos on and they would both dance for ages. If I ever tried to do any exercises they would both jump all over me, laughing and bashing me. Nothing was boring. They laughed all the time.

Once she was walking, Jordan was a very busy little girl, putting dirty nappies in the bin, moving things from room to room and peeling labels off tins in the cupboard. She would get a tissue if she sneezed, and if other people sneezed she would fetch them one too! One of the funniest things she did was to disappear into the bathroom then emerge into the hallway wrapped in and surrounded by toilet roll. Another favourite game was to sort out her nappies - she'd pull them out of the bag and throw them one by one over her shoulder. They'd go everywhere and she loved it.

She was also extremely affectionate, always kissing and cuddling. Sometimes she'd hold my face with her little hands, kiss me and say "Lufoo mummy". I just wanted to eat her - it was especially lovely because I never made her do it. Jordan was also very sensitive. If I cried or someone on television cried, she would too, with such a sad look on her face. She had an animated video of nursery rhymes, and when Humpty Dumpty fell off the wall she would jump and cry, really cry. She would be *so* sad everytime she saw it. I tried not playing the video but she really wanted to watch it, and I'd have to say "It's only pretend, he's okay really."

Bathtime was fun. She'd clean the bath with her

sponge, blow the bubbles, or tell me to. I'd say "Let me wash your hands" and she'd hold them out, or lift her arms if I said "Let me clean your armpits." She loved having a bath, cleaning her teeth, putting her pyjamas on and snuggling up on the settee to watch TV. Her favourite programmes were 'Only Fools & Horses', 'Star Trek', 'Darling Buds Of May' and 'Neighbours'. She especially liked Brad! She knew all the characters' names and would copy things they said.

I couldn't have asked for a lovelier daughter. Everyone who met her liked her immediately. She was so good, so caring, so affectionate, clever and beautiful.

early problems

Then things started to go wrong. Or rather, they had already started to, but no-one had put two-and-two together. Jordan had always suffered from numerous ear infections and so a few tests were done to measure the amount of fluid in her ears. She frequently had a high temperature, was quite 'vomity' and was on anti-biotics a lot. Some days Jordan had to be changed six or seven times; there was often so much mess that I would have to change my own clothes three times or more.

I had taken her to the Doctors and Health Visitors for all the things which concerned me, but the experts told me "Don't worry so much." One time, Jordan's ear had leaked a yellowy fluid overnight and at first I thought maybe her eardrum had burst. Obviously it hadn't or she would have been in excruciating pain, but no-one tried to work out what it was. It definitely wasn't ear wax. Even after this, I was still told "not to worry".

Around the time of Jordan's second birthday, she started to lose her balance for no apparent reason. Irregularly at first, then more and more often. The Health Visitors still didn't seem unduly worried, so I saw our Doctor who referred us to an Ear, Nose & Throat specialist. Some progress was finally made two weeks later when the ENT specialist said that Jordan had 'glue ear', a common complaint amongst children. Apparently, her right ear was full of fluid but she didn't seem to be losing her hearing. The specialist recommended inserting 'grommetts' into her ears to clear the infection and they would also remove the adenoids from her nose (enlarged tissue at the back of the nose that can sometimes hinder breathing). If that failed to resolve her balance problems, we would then have to see a Neurologist, because the cause of her difficulties would clearly have a more serious origin. I was very scared by the thought of surgery and was hoping that she only needed grommets.

Jordan coped unbelievably well. She never complained and was as good as ever. She was very wobbly first thing in the morning, but would improve after half an hour or so. With all this going on, she still became potty trained, she was brilliant. She had a few accidents but I assumed that was normal.

In October our Doctor made us an appointment to see a Paediatrician to decide if it was only her ears that we needed to worry about. Jordan was now getting embarrassed when she fell over, and not playing with other children so well as they made her jump and she would fall over. She preferred to sit quietly out of the way and watch them. She was not very steady on her feet and now refused to walk along walls holding my hand, something which she'd always loved to do.

In November we saw the Paediatrician, (not the one we were supposed to see, he had been called away), who said that she should be okay after her 'op' but booked us in for a check-up six weeks after that. He said that several things could have caused Jordan's problems, but he couldn't see any signs of them, not without X-rays anyway.

I was not happy. I was angry and scared. Jordan hadn't been right for some time and all the waiting was driving me nuts. I was afraid that I had been doing something wrong or not doing enough for her.

Hollie began following Jordan around to pick her up when she fell over and she would say "Up-a-daisy". Hollie became very protective towards her. It's funny the things children know without being told.

On January 25th, Jordan had her grommets put in and adenoids removed. We told her about going to hospital and that it would make her ears better and she accepted the situation very well.

Unfortunately, the Surgeon who performed the operation said he thought this was not the end of our problems but refused to elaborate. Instead, he recommended that we discuss things with a Paediatrician. I explained we were already seeing one and asked if I should bring the appointment forward but received the now familiar reply of "Don't worry".

I was very upset at this and in a way determined to prove him wrong, but at the same time I think I knew deep down that Jordan's problems couldn't be sorted out by grommets alone.

After the op, we couldn't go swimming and I had to be very careful when washing her hair, so as not to get any water in her ears. It took me a week just to pluck up the courage to even try. I coated some cotton wool in vaseline to plug her ears and I explained to her how careful we had to be.

Jordan was quite perky and looked well within a couple of days after the surgery, and her cheekiness soon returned - once when I wanted to show her something she said "Excuse me, I'm drawing!"

By February she couldn't walk without holding someone with both hands, her legs were very shaky and she was complaining of headaches. I tried to keep her legs exercised, thinking this would keep them strong for when her balance returned. It never did.

On 3rd March, we returned to the Paediatrician, this time seeing Mr Raffles, (whom we had originally been booked in to see). He was marvellous - he watched Jordan walk and play, did some reflex tests on her legs and feet and measured her head (which was large).

He said her ears had nothing to do with her walking. The problem appeared to be that for some reason the messages from her brain to the nerve endings in her feet were being blocked. Therefore, there must be pressure somewhere in the nervous system or brain area. There were many things it could be - he could only guess that it was probably fluid on the brain - 'hydracephalus'. If this was the case, it would be essential to find the cause, which sometimes was simple, sometimes not.

We were devastated. I cried and he apologised for upsetting me, but I was glad he was honest.

Mr. Raffles booked a scan for the 10th March. I tried to be optimistic during this time and to keep Jordan from seeing me cry or from feeling all our fears. I was dazed, like I'd had a blow to the head. I'm sure everyone else felt the same.

I wanted to be positive but my mind kept wondering to negative thoughts, then I'd look at Jordan playing or asleep, and in my head I'd be screaming "No, I won't let it be bad."

One of the Health Visitors phoned to ask what had happened and she said "I always knew it wasn't her ears." I was so angry - if she had known, why hadn't we been referred to someone earlier?

I'd been asking for help for so long and Jordan was missing out on so much, and that made me very angry. By now, she couldn't walk, catch or throw very well, she couldn't ride her bike and she couldn't run and jump. She was complaining of headaches most mornings.

Jordan's scan proved that there was indeed fluid on the brain. Quite a lot in fact. A blockage somewhere was stopping the fluid from circulating as it should, so it was building up.

I was told that the blockage was probably congenital, but that it was not tumorous.

The likely remedy was a 'shunt', which was a tube running from her brain to her abdomen, which would disperse the excess fluid and thus relieve the pressure, enabling the messages to get through to her nerve endings once again, which in turn would make her mobile once more. We'd be taught how to keep an eye on the shunt and Jordan should be able to live a 'normal' life. There would be few things she couldn't do. I cried with relief.

I began to feel a bit more positive. We had found what was wrong, we were doing something about it and all would be well.

We were booked in for admission to Great Ormond Street Hospital on Monday 14th March, for a more detailed scan and to probably have the shunt inserted.

Our telephone became a hotline, with lots of

concerned people asking about Jordan. After I'd repeated the news a dozen times it didn't seem so bad.

On the weekend prior to going to hospital, Jordan told me she had a 'headache in her knee'. On the Monday she woke up and said "I love you mummy" - she seemed to know she was going to hospital to get better and was chatty and bright. I thought we'd be in there for about ten days, so I decided to take Jordan's diary with me to record what happened. That way we could look back on it all as a bad time we had all got through.

Little did I know this was the beginning of the end, and the nightmare had only just begun.

the diary

Monday 14th March Day 1 of Jordan's hospital stay

Up at 5.30am. Pam and Jim arrived at 7.30am. Got to the hospital well before 9am. The Doctor s and Nurses on the ward are nice.

Dr Dan came to put a canula (an intravenous plastic tube used to give fluids or blood) in Jordan's feet to take some blood, but because of a problem with her veins he had trouble getting it in. Jordan got very upset, me too.

We were on the main ward all day, but got our own room tonight with a bathroom. Mum and Dad came this evening.

Jordan had a more detailed MRI scan this afternoon and was only slightly sedated. She was very good. It was so scary, being strapped into this big noisy machine, even her head was in there.

After a quick look at the scan, Dr Kumar, the Neurosurgeon, said he'd like to try to unblock Jordan's drainage system rather than just put a shunt in. He'll discuss it with the radiologist tomorrow and they will decide what to do. They possibly won't operate until Friday, but we're in good hands and we will just have to wait, if that's what it's going to take. A few more days won't make a lot of difference.

I have seen some awful sights today - it doesn't lessen Jordan's predicament, but there are some really sick children around.

Tuesday 15th March Day 2

Dr Kumar came to tell us the results of his discussion with the radiologist.

I heard the word "tumour" and it echoed around my head. I asked Dr. Kumar to stop and then asked Dad to take Jordan to the play room. I think he wanted to stay but I didn't want Jordan to see if I cracked up. There was a loud banging and buzzing in my head, I think I was crying. I couldn't hear my voice properly, but I said "Tumour? But we were told last week that there was nothing tumorous present?"

Devastation.

Dr. Kumar explained that it wouldn't have shown up properly on the less detailed first scan, but I shouldn't have been told it wasn't a tumour.

I know I said "I can't believe it." I was very angry and frightened and a hot pain spread throughout my body. I was shaking and felt sick. A tumour? My baby with a monster in her head. I have to build a pain protection barrier around myself - Jordan mustn't know how scared I am.

As soon as Kurt arrived I told him myself. I though that was best, I couldn't believe the words I was saying, that I was discussing our beautiful, perfect daughter.

She will be operated on at 8.30am tomorrow morning. They are going to try to remove the tumour as she is too small for radiotherapy. The tumour is big and it's rare, and they don't know why it is there. It is probably slow-growing and is blocking her drainage system. This is what has caused the hydracephalus, so it's got to be removed. It is going to be very risky because of Jordan's age and where it has grown. It will probably take three hours to complete surgery if everything goes to plan.

Inside the brain are four ventricles (spaces) through which passes the fluid that surrounds the brain. Because Jordan's tumour was in the third ventricle, the fluid couldn't pass through. When the skull fused over at around two years, there was no longer room for expansion inside the skull. So the trapped fluid had nowhere to go and instead just built up pressure on her brain.

Jordan's tumour was probably there from birth - it grew with her, but it wasn't until she was two when the skull fused that the problems became evident.

Jordan's eyes were checked this morning because she keeps rubbing them. The fluid is putting pressure on the back of her eyes, but that should go as the fluid lessens. They couldn't see any damage but she will be checked again after.

Dr Kumar wants to clear the blockage in one go and avoid putting in a shunt if at all possible. She'll have an external drain for a couple of days for excess fluid to escape. She might not look very pretty - it's a frontal operation, so her eyes and head could be swollen and bruised. Jordan is already on medicine to reduce internal head swelling from the operation.

We've just got to get through tomorrow. I can't imagine it. All the grandparents will be here, plus my brother Stuart and Kurt's brother Jamie.

Sally came. She bought Jordan an 'Aladdin' nightdress. Flowers arrived from my friends at the local college - everyone is so kind and concerned.

So many people will be thinking and praying for

Jordan tomorrow - let's hope it helps.

I can't explain how I feel. I'm numb - I've got to be strong for Jordan, I can't let it all out yet. I love Jordan so much and hate all this suffering she's going through. I just want her to be well and happy, I don't want a genius, just a healthy, happy child. Surely that's not too much to ask.

Wednesday 16th March Day 3: The Operation
Couldn't stop crying every time I looked at Jordan in the anaesthetic room. I really felt I wouldn't see her again.

I felt that I was betraying her by leaving her there with strangers, although she was 'out' when I left. I didn't feel like it was my body moving along the street. Sounds were muffled, I wasn't really aware of my surroundings, yet I was in so much pain. I could see it in Kurt's face, I don't know if it showed in mine. I didn't want to look.

I felt isolated, time didn't feel like it was moving at all. I felt I was in limbo, as if it was my life on the line.

Kurt and I and my cousin Jo went to have breakfast - it was like eating cardboard. We were only eating because we had to and the staff had said go out for a while. When we returned to the hospital lots of people visited and rang. The waiting was appalling, but Jordan finally came back after three hours, and didn't look as bad as I thought she would. They had shaved back about 6cm from her hairline and there was a scar over the top of her head from ear to ear. She was only allowed two people at the bed at one time. Jordan couldn't hold her drink down, so she had some small sponges on a stick to suck.

Jordan was full of tubes and there was blood in her hair which was all stuck together, but who cares? She came back and is alert and aware of her surroundings.

Saturday 19th March Day 6
Cliff rang from Bermuda, and many other people too. Debbie came with her Mum and brought Jordan a woolly penguin and comics, plus some cards from play-school. Friends also brought balloons, teddies, clothes, sweets and food. Charlton rang and sent a card.

The Nurses and Doctor s have been great. They say Jordan is doing very well - she had a bit of a temperature but it came down. She is taking painkillers and is on steroids to reduce internal swelling. She had started eating and drinking on Thursday evening and on Friday had another scan.

The results of this showed that Jordan's ventricles are more of a normal size. But there is more fluid around the brain, apparently to be expected whilst the ventricles and brain settle to a more normal size. Dr Kumar is pleased because Jordan's brain fluid now seems to be doing what it should.

The consultant Mr Hayward is also pleased. He got at least 95% of the tumour out although some had to be left in as it wasn't clear whether it was brain or tumour tissue. If the tests are negative the major difficulties are over, although she still may have to have a shunt. If not, things are far more complicated, because she's too small for radiotherapy.

She was disconnected from the drip this morning, although the canula in her foot was left in until tomorrow at least, in case it's needed again.

Last night was awful. Jordan was in a lot of pain. I got to bed at midnight and was called at 1am - she was on the main ward, which is not quite Intensive Care, but they can keep a better eye on her there than in our room. She was screaming "Oh, mummy" and holding her head - it was awful. Back to bed at 3am.

Sunday 20th March Day 7

Up at 7am. Jordan was sick twice in the night and had to have her dressing changed - her external drain is leaking a lot.

Today she was sick a few times. Her lemon squash came back up pink, so she's on fluid only, little and often. If it stays down she can start to eat again. If not, a drip will be required again for fluids to replace what she's losing.

Jordan's so tired, so I've asked for no visitors tomorrow, for her sake.

We're lucky Jordan is still here, so I hope no-one's offended. A couple of days break will do everyone some good and she can try to sleep.

I love her so much. I want the test results to come through quickly.

Monday 21st March Day 8

Jordan kept her fluids down last night and for breakfast but then she had to stop feeding because she is going to be sedated to have her drain removed.

Cliff rang again and lots of cards have arrived. People are so caring.

Jordan has slept well all morning, poor baby. I am dreading the drain removal. She was sedated at 1.40pm and the drain removed. They stitched the hole and she didn't seem too distressed.

Her bandage is gone, she has eaten and drunk a fair bit, and is very sleepy . I would like the canula in her foot to be taken out now.

The sound of frightened children is awful, I really have to try to shut it out.

It's been a nice quiet day. Jordan has slept a lot, helped by the sedation. She is so brave, accepting and trusting, but I don't know how much she understands or will remember. I hope not too much.

We will get the test results tomorrow.

Tuesday 22nd March Day 9 The Best Day
Jordan's tumour is benign! I'm *not* going to lose my baby. The relief is so immense I could have fainted. I felt like jelly and had a good cry. When Mr Hayward said the word "benign", I felt like a great weight had been lifted from me. I had the same thumping in my head as when I was first told about the tumour. I was so excited. I rang a few people and told Sally "My baby is not going to die."

Jordan's temperature went up and we spent all afternoon trying to get it down. I was frantic. I kept thinking she was taking one step forward and two steps back. Fortunately, by this evening her temperature was back down again.

I don't know how I will ever thank everyone for their support, there is no way we could have managed without it. More cards and cuddly toys, some from people I don't know, but who are all thinking of Jordan.

Being here and seeing Jordan and all these other kids suffering, makes me wonder how anyone can believe in a 'god'. Sorry Jordan, but seeing you and the other children makes me feel this way.

Sally said that the whole atmosphere has changed since we found out the tumour was benign - I am so happy and feel so relaxed. I'm glad that Jordan doesn't know the fear that we do as adults.

Maybe that's why she's so resilient.

Jordan kept saying "Where is Kurt's brother?" over and over, meaning Jamie. She kept repeating herself and I kept repeating the answer - she was like a little tape machine gone wrong. Then out of the blue she said "I've got a brain". She's obviously taken in the conversations going on around her.

Wednesday 23rd March Day 10
Jordan was sick this morning and had a high temperature again. The Doctors feel it's probably due to the blood left over from the surgery still in the brain fluid - until it disperses she could be up and down. I hope it is what they say.

She'll have the staples in her head wound removed tomorrow, and she'll also be scanned again. I hope everything is working properly.

She perked up a bit this afternoon.

A little boy called Rowan, who had his tumour removed the same day as Jordan, has had some bad news - his tumour was malignant and now they've found another one, which is inoperable. He can only have chemotherapy. The malignancy is unpredictable and there are no guarantees. His family is devastated, as we all are.

Thursday 24th March Day 11

Kurt stayed with Jordan last night and I had a night away on staff recommendation.

Today she had double sedation for her scan and staple removal - all 31 of them. She got in a state asking for me in the scanning room, so by the time I'd got there she'd had a second lot of sedation. This caused her to sleep for three or four hours afterwards and I also caught an hour of sleep.

More cards and pressies and one from Bill, a male Nurse who was here for a week.

Jordan's temperature had gone up and blood tests showed her white cell count was up, which means there is an infection somewhere. They'll have to get a urine sample - she has a bag placed over the appropriate area to collect the urine. She has drunk a little and eaten a few grapes and has now gone back to sleep again

One step forward and two steps back.

Friday 25th March Day 12

Jordan slept until 2am and was then restless until the morning. Her temperature has shot up again and she hasn't been to the toilet since yesterday morning. One of the consultants felt her bladder and you could see her abdomen was full, so she had to have a catheter tube to empty it. Stuart and I went for breakfast while Dad watched Jordan.

She has been in bed all this time and I miss her cuddling me even though I can cuddle and kiss her all the time and tell her how much I love her.

She has a urinary infection which will be treated with anti-biotics and hopefully that will do it. The scan results were good - her ventricles are back to normal. No sign of hydracephalus - touch wood, no shunt please.

She is very sleepy, probably because of the infection, but we have to keep her fluid intake going.

I was so worried because she had big bags under her eyes. She looked frail and helpless, and was hardly able to speak. She ate two biscuits dunked in coffee and drank some lemonade.

She got Easter eggs, clothes and a hat from Pam.

While we walked some friends back to the car, Jordan's bowels and bladder let rip and the bed was flooded - when we got back she'd been washed and changed.

She is very quiet and calm but looks so sad, it's heartbreaking.

Saturday 26th March Day 13

Jordan had a massive seizure last night. She went as stiff as a board and her arms and legs were waving about slowly, like seaweed. Her eyes were looking to the left and she couldn't hear us - it was horrific. I kept saying to her "Don't be scared" but I think she was. I was terrified. My stomach felt like lead, I felt panic rising through me - what on earth was happening? The tumour was gone - why was her body doing this? What sort of infection could cause this reaction?

She had a scan at about 2am (still no sign of hydracephalus) followed by a lumbar puncture for which the results will take about two days. A lumbar puncture is when an amount of the fluid that surrounds the brain and spinal column is withdrawn using a syringe. The patient has to curl up in a ball while the needle is inserted between a couple of vertebrae. This is then tested for infections and abnormalities.

She is now on three types of strong anti-biotics and painkillers, as well as blood plasma to spread the heat in her body more evenly - her hands and feet are cold whilst her body is on fire. Apparently, this is because the extremities give up their heat to the body because the major organs need it.

She's probably had an infection in her head, as well as a urinary one. It has been awful - I don't know how much she can take. She has fought so hard, but I hope she has enough left for the rest of the struggle.

Jordan's been fairly stable today although she hasn't come round. Her heartbeat has been a bit irregular, but the Doctor was not overly worried.

I have been kissing her and telling her I love her, I hope she realises it. I lost it a bit today, but I can't be controlled all the time.

Sunday 27th March Day 14
Bad day. I was awoken by a Nurse at 6.30am because Jordan was asking for me, but by the time I got there she was going back to sleep. At first, she seemed better, then not so good later. In the end they put in an urgent external drain again.

Her scan showed more fluid build-up in one of the ventricles, so hydracephalus has reared its ugly head after all. This could mean more surgery under general anaesthetic.

Now Jordan will probably need a shunt, but this can only be inserted once the infection has cleared up, and her fluid pressure has evened out. She is out for the count on Codeine and has her own nurse.

One of the Nurses popped in even though she has finished work for nine days. Pam and Jim stayed overnight, Dad and Mum came, and Sally also popped in for a while. I have some good friends.

I feel detached. Jordan had to have half of her head shaved for the drain. I think I will have to crop her hair or she'll look funny. It's strange how silly things can seem important. She'll still look gorgeous. How much more can my baby take? I only want her to be able to run and walk and be happy.

The wound on Jordan's head has opened up, so they've put a stitch in the end.

Very late on this evening, I spoke to another Neurologist and said I wanted to know the truth, everything. That is how I cope, by knowing and learning about what is going on and trying to understand.

Jordan has (1) Surgical meningitis (2) The fluid from the inside and outside of the brain is conflicting and causing a lot of pressure (3) Her body temperature is wrong - it's called peripheral shut-down. Her feet are now wrapped in bubble wrap and blankets and she's being given blood plasma to even the temperature out. They're draining off a bit of fluid quite quickly then slowing it down. The meningitis is already being treated by the anti-biotics she's on. They've suspected it for a couple of days - I just wish I had been told, I need honesty.

Poor baby. She has got a real fight on her hands. I can barely look at her, it's like Jordan has gone away and she is someone else. Her hands and feet are bruised and full of holes from constant blood tests and moving the canulas.

The two drips she had in her right arm have packed up, her veins just couldn't take anymore. So it has been moved to her left hand, but because her hands are so cold her veins are contracted and not easy to get into. I feel lost and so alone, although there are so many people that care. It's my baby and she is going through hell. I would love to take it all away. I just don't want her to suffer anymore. If there is anyone watching over her, I just wish they would ease her pain, or tell me how to. She doesn't deserve this at all - she's never hurt anyone, she only brings joy and she is so gorgeous inside and out.

My angel, I love her so much.

Monday 28th March Day 15
This morning Jordan recognised me - what a wonderful feeling. She is fairly stable although her temperature is still up.

One of the Doctors told me that as Meningitis is an inflammation of the Meninges (surrounding the brain), if it goes down that might reduce the fluid pressure and possibly avoid the need for a shunt.

Feeling helpless.

Pam and Jim stayed - I slept from about 1am to 8.15am. Jordan had a good night, though her urine and tears are stained an orangey colour from all the anti-biotics.

Thursday 31st March Day 18
I have been too tired to write the last couple of days.

On Tuesday night Jordan's temperature was

playing up again. She has an external drain for her brain fluid and a drip going into her abdomen, called a femoral line. This is to get her fluids through to prevent any dehydration.

Yesterday I left the hospital with my brother Stuart and came back this morning.

Jordan and I got an electric shock on our lips when I kissed her. She is not sleeping. She had a scan and X-ray today. Her temperature is still up and we need to know why. Her ventricles are still large, the outside fluid is less. She may have a shunt on Saturday when they take the external drain out. More tests today.

I got upset today, when I thought she was going to have another fit. I was so worried. Debbie the Nurse was very understanding. If only we could find the cause of this temperature problem we could treat it.

So Jordan is still in a bad way but communicating well. She ate half a banana and half a slice of bread and butter. I had to break bits off and put them in her mouth but she ate them, so that is good.

Jordan told me "I'm not very well and I love you" and she also said that Beth the Nurse was naughty! She's so funny, she really likes Beth.

We have to take it one day at a time.

Got pressies from a couple of mums at the playgroup. Finally got her temperature down to normal at 7.30pm and she went to sleep. How long will it last? How long will her temperature stay down? How much more must she endure before she can get better?

I forgot to mention that the other day Jordan got a Certificate Of Bravery which all the Nurses have been signing for her.

This is a hell on earth that I wouldn't wish on my worst enemy. I am not coping so well now. I break down a lot, but Jordan doesn't see it. She's so brave, and I have to be the same for her.

Friday 1st April Day 19
Dad and Mum came today. Had lunch with Dad while Mum watched Jordan.

Jordan is bright on and off. She slept well last night but she's tired today. I had an hour's sleep today. We had Beth as Nurse today - she's so good, always trying to make Jordan as comfortable as possible.

They won't operate tomorrow, Jordan isn't well enough. They've found another bug in the brain fluid and changed her anti-biotics to cover it.

Still not much change physically, although Jordan looks better facially. I don't know how she does it. She's fought so hard, she's even been eating and drinking today. Strange how the body works, but very clever. I hope Jordan can keep fighting.

Saturday April 2nd Day 20
She's still got a temperature and her arms are really stiff. Beth and I worked on Jordan's arms and legs and got them a bit looser.

She has to sleep with her legs bent, as they seem not to stiffen up so much that way.

She asked for a cuddle, so she got one, but I can tell she's very frightened.

I can't believe it's Easter weekend, it's so quiet and awful for Jordan, she's so fed up.

Jordan ate a Weetabix for breakfast, and some mince and potatoes and ice-cream. She also drank some juice. Lots of runny nappies, and the bed got flooded again. Her poo was a rusty colour today, which must be the anti-biotics.

Easter Sunday 3rd April Day 21
Jordan's temperature was up and down again all night. I washed her hair with a sponge and then cut the longer bits. Jordan got agitated and her wound started to leak - we took the plaster off at the end of her scar and found a big soft lump that moved when you touched it and more liquid came out.

Ian the Charge Nurse took a swab and squeezed the rest out. Could this be the reason for the unstable temperature? I hope so, at least we'll know more of what's going on.

Jordan got a teddy and an Easter egg from The Parrot Ward, and some teddies, books and more eggs from friends.

She livened up this evening, laughing at Beth pretending to strangle Dad. She was really laughing. It was lovely. Then suddenly, her bowels exploded again all over the bed.

Jordan seems fed up and depressed, she must be so bored in bed all this time. We must try to liven things up tomorrow.

I don't feel that there's too much progress, apart from when her temperature is down, which isn't very often unfortunately.

I've been taking Jordan's temperature every hour and charting it. I gave her some medicine through her nasal gastric tube today. I had to draw out a small amount of stomach contents through it first with a syringe, and test that on a piece of litmus paper. If the paper turns pink, the tube is in the right place in the stomach. You then give the medicine down the tube and flush it all down with the stomach contents. It was easy, although not a nice thing to do to my baby, but I need to be involved. I'll earn my nurse's uniform yet!

The Doctors say "sit tight and see what happens".

Surgery probably on Wednesday. Yuk, poor baby.

Monday 4th April Day 22

Jordan's external drain is to be removed and her femoral line replaced by a drip going into her neck - a femoral line can easily become infected. Maybe this could explain her temperature problems.

Turned out to be a very long and strange day. Jordan was quiet all day, she looked beautiful and almost pleading. She actually burst into tears a few times for no apparent reason.

Then I knew Jordan was going into a fit - her eyes went to the right and wouldn't come back, they flickered slightly, she only responded to her earlobe being pinched. I wasn't sure if Jordan could hear us and not respond, or if she couldn't hear us at all.

The first fit lasted for 45 minutes, there was a five minute break and then she went into another one, not violent or shaking, just eye deviation and not being with us.

She was given some drugs to relax her then taken into surgery.

I can't get used to the anaesthetic room and her going under, it's like saying goodbye and giving her away to have pain inflicted. I feel so awful, I hope she's not too aware of these things.

When she came back from surgery she looked okay but frightened - I hate that look, I don't want her to be afraid. Jordan slipped into a lovely sleep but it didn't last long and she spent the night as before, drifting. Today's problems may be related to the major seizure last week, rather than an on-going epileptic problem.

The drain is out but her neckline looks awful. She has still got socks and gloves on to keep her peripheral temperatures up.

Tuesday 5th April Day 23
The consultant has asked for someone from Infectious Diseases to take some blood tests from Jordan to see if there's an infection they can't find here. They're doing their best.

I've been told that her tumour was sited in an area that controls the temperature so the fluctuations could be from the removal.

Poor baby, things just don't seem to be getting any better. She's so strong and so brave. Jordan's also on an anti-fungal drug now to prevent thrush of the mouth, which can be caused by anti-biotics.

Everyone here is known as a Mum or Dad of a child, for example, Jordan's Mum. It all revolves around the child's names.

All the parents seem to counsel each other, it's a big help to talk to one another.

They've put Jordan on to two anti-convulsants, and she'll be on at least one of them for three months. After that, we'll have to see. She's drinking and had some bread and butter and baby dessert and she seemed to like that.

Debbie came, we went for some fish and chips

while Kurt watched Jordan. She seems quite tired, but we'll see how it goes.

Wednesday 6th April Day 24
Jordan slept quite well. I changed and washed her and changed the bed first thing. The Infectious Diseases registrar came and I got the feeling that she wanted me to say Jordan was improving, but she's not.

Today she's having a lumbar puncture, another scan and an eye test.

4.15pm. Just waiting now. She's not eaten since 2pm - shouldn't be long now. Mum phoned.

I can't bear to think of Jordan having another lumbar puncture, but I suppose it's necessary otherwise they wouldn't do it. Poor little honey. I've been showing Beth some Christmas photos of Jordan, she really liked them.

She finally got scanned after 7pm. There is a small mass at the front of her brain, probably a post-operative collection of blood, which will be checked out in the morning. So no lumbar puncture until we know for sure.

Thursday 7th April Day 25
Jordan woke about 10am and had her lumbar puncture around lunchtime. The Doctor who did it tried and failed about three times. He blamed the needles, but he's not a permanent member of staff. Another Doctor came and did it first time. Jordan cried and screamed so much. The way she looked at me was heartbreaking. She had no sedation because she had had some yesterday, it was awful. Her nose

bled because she got into such a state.

She slept for a while but it's midnight now and she's not sleeping. Jordan won't speak. The lumbar puncture has affected her badly. She is eating and drinking little but often.

Last night 'Mork & Mindy' was on television, Jordan smiled and said "Nanu Nanu" and, still smiling, dropped off to sleep. A wonderful reaction but we've had nothing since.

She got hot again tonight, it must be driving her crazy, it is me. I was really cheesed off today, so it was good to have Mum here. I opened Jordan's Easter presents - more bunnies but she's not very interested.

Friday 8th April Day 26
Jordan and I didn't sleep well last night. She was crying and making whimpering noises which is not like her at all. I'm sure it was the trauma of yesterday. She ate Weetabix and a few mouthfuls of toast this morning.

I put Jordan in the buggy and went up to the sixth floor where the corridor is covered by a glass dome. The sun was shining, it was lovely and Jordan fell asleep. I went out in the sun for a while.

A Nurse took some stool samples because of Jordan's diarrhoea - she hates being pulled about and I don't blame her. Jordan went into a fit for ten minutes, then she came out of it for ten minutes and then back into another fit - she was given some drugs and then slept.

Jordan may well have an infection of the brain tissue......what next?

Apparently, it's very difficult for anti-biotics to get

through to the brain tissue, so the dose has to be increased. If this doesn't work, Jordan could have an operation to wash her brain with anti-biotics, but at the moment she isn't strong enough for this.

Kurt came and Dad gave me a lift home to have a night off. We won't have her left alone overnight. I hate to leave her, but it's good to see different scenery and people for a while.

Saturday 9th April Day 27
I phoned the hospital and Jordan had had another fit last night, but was now peaceful.

I hate being away but I am desperately tired and even being rained on today felt good. Went to Mum's for lunch and Dad's this evening. I dreamt of Jordan all night.

Sunday 10th April Day 28
Jordan had another fit yesterday. When I got back to hospital, Jordan gave me a lovely smile, but she really had to make a huge effort to do it.

Jordan ate and drank over the weekend, but when I tried to feed her she could do neither, not even through a straw or from the bottle. She's not speaking either. My head feels like it's exploding. How much more can she take?

I'll probably have to wait until tomorrow lunchtime to get any answers. We're sliding backwards. It's nobody's fault but I want to know the facts, what's going on? Jordan had her medication through her nasal tube and we put her in the buggy for a change and gave her a little milk feed down her tube, but she vomited and went into a fit.

So she had to have the anti-convulsants in suppository form because of the vomiting. Her temperature is up and she had another small fit at 10.40pm. At 11.55pm she went into one long fit where she would doze for a couple of seconds then fit again.

Had Paraldehyde rectally, which smells like paint-stripper, but she poo'ed it all out. I wish she could relax and sleep. She did finally drop off.

Jordan now has to take nine types of drug every day. I want to get a list of them all and what they each do, so that we'll never forget.

Monday 11th April Day 29
I am distraught. The consultant said that meningitis could have caused thrombosis in the veins around the brain, which in turn could be causing the fits.

Who knows?

Jordan is not herself at all, she's just gone downhill. I can't bear it, it's like Jordan has gone away. She doesn't seem to know me, apart from my smile yesterday.

Dad came, he bought lunch and dinner and said I was grumpy. I think I'm entitled to be grumpy.

I was very tired tonight. I can't bear to watch my baby suffer, that's if she is. I don't know what she's thinking or how she feels. I just hope she'll never remember this.

This is a living nightmare, one you could never imagine yourself because it is just too awful. It tears me apart. I can't imagine how Jordan feels or what she's thinking. I really hope she has no idea.

She is still so beautiful, even though her eyes are staring, her arms waving about, her legs twitching and her bowels spasming.

Where has my baby gone? How long before I get her back again? In what condition?

It doesn't matter in what condition, as long as she's happy and healthy and can walk and run and be 'normal' - that's not too much to ask.

I don't want this for me but for Jordan. She's got so much catching up to do with enjoying herself, so much lost fun to make up for. I hope she's going to have loads.

Tuesday 12th April Day 30
Jordan was vomiting in the night and then retching when there was nothing to vomit. She is going to have surgery, a half shunt, which will allow them to take small amounts of fluid away for testing, a process called 'tapping'.

Jordan's operation was at 12.30 last night. She had a couple of eye deviation fits before the operation but she couldn't have any drugs. She came back after two hours and seemed okay although quite hot.

She is 'Nil By Mouth' and can't eat or drink. She can't keep anything in when given rectally and didn't sleep until this morning.

The dietician is coming to see Jordan tomorrow. They will have to feed her intravenously to build up her loss of calories, she's so thin.

She had a couple more convulsive fits. She arches her neck and makes a funny noise, poor baby.

She had some drugs rectally which stayed put, so she calmed down.

I can't see an end to this for Jordan. It just doesn't seem fair, what did she do? She doesn't deserve this at all. It's horrific. I'm not sure what she knows, I just hope it's not enough for her to be distressed or scared, or worried about being unable to communicate. The idea is too awful for words.

Thursday 14th April Day 32
Jordan slept all night and focussed on the Nurses doing her intravenous drugs this morning. Then she had a fit, not violent, but she was arching her neck, rolling her eyes and making a strange sound again. I pinched her earlobe and there was no response, so I know she had gone far away. She seemed to come back for a while and then went to sleep.

Jordan had an EEG the other day, which measures brain activity - it showed 'mild activity'. I don't know what this means.

Debbie says that Chloe pretends to talk to Jordan on the phone at home, saying "Hello, are you better? Are you still in hospital?"

They couldn't do another EEG because her head moves about too much to get a true reading. They are waiting to test her urine, so they can see what's needed in her special feed - called Total Parental Nutrition or TPN - this goes straight into her body through a special tube, and is custom made for each child's exact needs.

Jordan is having more blood plasma because she's still peripherally cold. There are so many complications, if only we could get one or two under control it would be great.

At 11pm she had another fit.

If her feed is started tomorrow and we can keep her temperature down, then maybe she'll start to improve on Monday - that's my idea. Let's hope so. We've got to got forward now, no more going backwards. I'm not so depressed today.

Jordan's eyes seem a bit livelier, she's focussed a couple of times, but not often. A bit more every day is all we can hope for.

Friday 15th April Day 33

Jordan got her TPN tonight - at last, she might put on some weight. Her white cell count is down which may mean her anti-biotics being stopped.

Jordan has a rash on her face, trunk and the top of her arms, so we're being isolated in our room as a precaution....oh goody!!

Sunday 17th April Day 35

I had the weekend off trying to relax but it's hard to sleep and my dreams are full of Jordan running and laughing in fields of long grass and flowers.

I'm now on the way back to the hospital, having been delayed by roadworks and diversions. I'm getting worried and distressed about Jordan. I'm taking my Terence Trent D'Arby tape to the hospital for her - the song she likes best is 'She Kisses Me There'. She always asks me to play it in the car.

Jordan had a fit yesterday morning and apparently her rash is not much better. I'll find out for myself soon enough.

On arrival I found my baby no different, and her rash only slightly better. Kurt thinks her rash is typical of a German measles rash - a possibility? Jordan has started a new movement where her right arm and shoulder twitch a few times in a row and then stop. She doesn't seem to be fitting though.

Brian and Anne came on Saturday and bought Jordan a big fluffy duck, and a parent who had left the ward phoned to ask how Jordan was! Everyone is being so kind, I don't know how we'll ever pay them back.

My poor baby still doesn't respond to me, but I'll keep talking and reading and playing tapes, trying to get through.

Monday 18th April Day 36 (five weeks so far)
6pm Jordan has been focusing on me! Lots of times! She seems fairly lucid. It's wonderful.

She's not wearing nappies because her bottom is so sore, she's laying on a very large nappy so the air can get to her.

Jordan is going to have her Femoral line changed to a Hickman line which is bigger, deeper and can stay in longer. People who have chemotherapy have Hickman lines.

Her rash is still bad and is now down her legs and back. She protested whilst having physio and we changed her bedding.

She now has a Spenko mattress, it's soft and quilted like a sleeping bag, because she's lying down all the time and it prevents her getting sore. Her arms and legs are so tense this evening. Her left eye reacts quicker to light than the right one, which remains sluggish.

Tuesday 19th April Day 37
Lots of diarrhoea in the night and this morning. She's not so sore as they are using some ointment on her

and it's excellent.

At about 2pm she went to theatre for the operation to insert the Hickman line. After the surgery I got her sorted out, but we only allowed one other person by the bed other than me for Jordan's sake.

The Hickman line goes into the right atrium of the heart and can stay in there for up to a year, but we won't need it that long. Kaz, a fellow patient, went home today. We no longer know anyone here, we've become the long term 'inmates'. It's really strange.

A Nurse bought Jordan a little present, even though she was told not to get too attached. I wasn't very pleased when I heard this - I understand the concern under normal circumstances, but I need to be attached to people, to have consistency, and I think it's good for Jordan, no matter how little she seems to be aware. I'm not unduly concerned because there are no unhealthy attachments going on. The Nurses are so wonderful, they're so caring, far more than duty calls for. Dad bought a load of chocolate bars for them.

I am feeling reasonably positive today. Will Jordan ever forgive me for sometimes getting so low that I don't have much hope? I hope so. It's just from being so tired, feeling helpless, watching my baby being so poorly and everyone being so baffled.

Wednesday 20th April Day 38
She slept well last night and only needed changing a couple of times. She's still alert. Nurse Lisa thought Jordan said "No" when she was doing something to her. I hope so. She definitely gets the hump when she's moved about. We sat her up for a bit.

The consultant says he's pleased with her progress

at the moment.

They don't know what the rash was, they're not always sure of everything. I'm sure that Jordan tried to speak when Kurt came, her face looked animated and her mouth moved as though she was going to say something. Jamie thought that she looked better today.

So it's just a matter of time again. Day by day.

11pm Jordan's temperature is up again, and she seems a bit depressed and is making noises. I'm a bit worried. Please, no more setbacks.

Jordan had a scan today and there was some misunderstanding about the exact placement of the injection, but luckily I am well up to date on her condition and we were able to sort it out.

Corne says I could contact her if I wasn't happy about anything. Jordan is crying out more when she's moved about, she seems very fed up.

Friday 22nd April Day 40
Jordan had a test to check for an infection of the heart but thankfully they didn't find anything.

Kaz, a child who had been in for surgery a few weeks previously, came in for a check-up. He gave Jordan a kiss and wished her better and said he hoped we wouldn't be here for his next check-up. He said we'd been here long enough. Not bad for an eight year old.

Sunday 24th April Day 42
Yesterday was my brother Stuart's birthday. I couldn't celebrate with him because it didn't feel right without Jordan there. I've really missed her and have been

looking at baby photos. It's heartbreaking. I saw a few children over the weekend and feel quite detached when I see them running around, climbing and laughing.

Why Jordan? Not that I'd wish this on anyone else, but why does she have to go through all this? She's never hurt a fly. We can only hope that she'll come through this as completely as possible with a decent quality of life and be as healthy and happy as possible.

Jordan has now got 87 "Get Well" cards. She's been fitting again. Every now and then all her limbs raise themselves and lower again several times and then stop. Her brain fluid pressure is now normal, but her temperature is up again - why?

I'm just busy trying to cool her down.

The Nurses are all concerned about her. We seem to have come to a standstill. There do not seem to be any answers.

Woke up just before 2am and Jordan was crying and fitting. I don't know if she gets cramp in her legs when they straighten out and stiffen while she fits...I don't know anything. More rectal drugs at 2.25am, poor baby.

Are we going backwards? It's getting on my nerves. What's going on? How much more can she take? I don't like these fits, they exhaust Jordan, but she still can't sleep properly, and being so tired must be dragging her down.

Jordan is definitely bulking up on the TPN. Her tummy doesn't cave inwards anymore.

Monday 25th April Day 43

Corne is going to re-run all the tests. There is something that they can't find. Jordan is a mystery, and it's so frustrating.What has she got to endure?

I can't stop crying. I feel helpless and hopeless and furious. I want to shake everyone into action, but what can they do if they don't know what's going on? Lunchtime - I bathed Jordan in bed and massaged some baby lotion in. The skin under her arms just peeled off in strips, after having built up over the weekend. Tasha the physio has been, Jordan didn't moan much.

4pm - I asked for more drugs because the fitting seems to be going on and on. She seems to be asleep but still has spasms. Her temperature has been up and down, it's mad. I always say it but how much more can she take?

The microbiologist Andrew advised a return to anti-biotics. I gave my approval because I didn't want to wait any longer. At last some action!

I am pleased she's back on anti-biotics as the blood tests have shown there's an infection somewhere.

Tuesday 26th April Day 44

Jordan's in a bad way. Constantly fitting, no drugs worked until 4am and then she slept a while.

Jordan's also been on oxygen. I spoke to the consultant this morning and said that I felt Jordan was worse than ever and that I couldn't stand to see her deterioration anymore. Not knowing what was going on is the most distressing part. He was very understanding, so she'll be scanned today and some sort of decision will be made. I've made it clear that whatever it's possible to do, I want done - there must be something that someone can do!

I don't now if Jordan can take much more, her body must be exhausted. Her major organs must be overworked and she's getting no exercise (apart from physio) so I don't want anymore of this going from day to day stuff. I want action now!!! For Jordan's sake, she's just got progressively worse, especially so in the last 48 hours.

11.45pm - Jordan eventually got her scan this afternoon. The Doctor said there was nothing obvious and that we'd have to wait for the anti-biotics to work.

I went crazy. I said that I didn't want to wait, that maybe Jordan couldn't afford to wait, something had to be done. He said that the consultant from Infectious Diseases would also look at the scan and give his opinion but not until tomorrow.

I said that wasn't good enough - I was furious. The Infectious Diseases consultant came but the scans had got stuck in the machine whilst he was trying to read them - what a farce!

Got another card from, Rosina - 89 now!

Jordan's face was swollen because she has reacted to one of the anti-biotics, so she will be given an anti-histamine before each dose in future.

The Infectious Diseases consultant will discuss Jordan with another consultant tomorrow - "That will have to do" I screamed and I cried, now I'll have to wait. Dr Dan was reassuring and maybe it will be better to let them all get their heads together and sort out a proper plan of action. Jordan definitely needs that.

A couple of Nurses came in to see how we are - news travels fast, especially bad news.

It is 1.50am and Jordan is red all over. Her temperature is high and her skin is peeling from her hands and feet, while her whole body is puffy, including her hands, legs and ankles.

Every time I wonder "what else can happen?" something does. My poor baby is ravaged. Dr Dan is on call tonight which is reassuring. Everyone is so caring and trying so hard but Jordan's body is having none of it. I brought her playschool photo in this week, everyone loved it.

I cut Jordan's hair today, like a crop - it looks better and may keep her head cooler. I'll try anything.

Dad didn't leave until late. We went out to eat - I now feel safe leaving Jordan just for an hour with the Nurses, they're so good. Dad's been such a support today. She's had just about every complication going. Dr Dan said I should get some sleep because Jordan will need me tomorrow.

Wednesday 27th April Day 45
It has been decided that Jordan will have surgery. They will open the original scar to look underneath. Surgery was at 6pm so Pam took me for a pizza. Jordan was back at 7.30pm - she's got through yet another surgery!

They removed the bone flap that was previously taken away to get to the tumour. There was a collection of 'mucky stuff' underneath which was removed and the area cleaned. The muck was sent for testing. The bone flap was not replaced.

The piece of bone is about 7cm square, back from

Jordan's forehead. It was cleaned and frozen, to possibly be replaced at a later date. It was kept out in case it carried any germs. I understand why the bone has not been replaced, but it seems like one strange thing after another. After all she's been through it's most humiliating for her.

Jordan was very shaky after surgery and seemed frightened. I calmed her down by talking to her and stroking her, but she was still very hot and swollen.

By 1.30am, even though her temperature was high, she was sound asleep and very relaxed, even her arms and legs. Even when she was turned every couple of hours she just opened her eyes, moaned a little and went straight back to sleep - it was almost too good to be true!

Thursday 28th April Day 46
The consultant came around and said that the collection of pus wasn't very big behind the bone flap. He seemed surprised that Jordan looked so well and that her temperature seemed good. She's slept and been relaxed and cool. She protests by crying out when anything is done to her.

I'm getting the impression that Jordan may well have long-term problems and will never be 100% again. I don't mind as long as she has some quality of life, is not in pain, and can be happy and enjoy things.

The results of Jordan's EEG came today. They show that Jordan's strange movements are not fits but "dystonic" movements. The nerve endings in her brain are damaged from surgery or infection, and are sending incorrect messages to the rest of her body. The movements are involuntary and Jordan is unaware of them.

When she does wake up properly she may be able to override them with voluntary movements. If not, there are drugs that can help.

Corne and I had a chat. She says that Jordan has been comatose for some time. All her reactions are reflexive responses to noises and such like. She's locked away somewhere inside her head.

Friday 29th April Day 45

Last night Jordan only cried out when her nappy was being changed. Nurse Lisa drew little pictures all over Jordan's nappies to pretty them up.

Corne said Microbiology had phoned - the pus contained lots of dead germs which had stayed in there without being able to multiply, because of the drugs.

The ward sister Lindy and I had a chat about Jordan's condition. At its most basic her problems are as follows:

1. *Comatose* - unconscious, non-responsive. She will come out of it when she's ready.
2. *Dystonic movements.*
3. *Temperature control.*

I try to help Jordan's temperature by tepid sponging, using a sponge and warm water, almost like a bed bath. When the water evaporates from the skin it takes heat away with it, helping to reduce her temperature.

Lindy told staff about our little chat concerning how Jordan may be left when this is all over, so that everyone knows what the situation is.

It's so warm up here, the weather is beautiful and sunny outside. It was lovely this evening, and we've got two fans in our room now.

We've still got to take things one day at a time really. Waking up properly is up to Jordan.

She's fought so hard. I was kissing her on the lips today and she was making a little moaning noise, so I kissed her again and I was saying "Oh, alright, just one more" between kisses. One time her lips parted and made a little smacking noise. Was she trying to kiss me back? I hope so. I'll play this game all the time, we used to play it and I like it!

Jordan cried tonight even though we weren't doing anything to her. Maybe she was bored? Was she trying to tell us how she feels?

Although she always looks lovely, when she's asleep and peaceful she looks exceptionally beautiful, so like a baby, innocent and gorgeous. It's lovely to see her so peaceful. She looks as though there's nothing wrong with her at all - IF ONLY!!! I love her so much, it breaks my heart. If only I could take it all away I would.

Tuesday 2nd May Day 51

Jordan's not sleeping and she cried in the night. Again, I don't know why. I keep kissing her on the lips, I'm sure she moves her lips up to mine ever so slightly and makes funny noises in her throat.

Wednesday 4th May Day 52

Rosina phoned today and is still sending lovely cards - Jordan now has over 93!

Jordan hasn't slept too well and she's been crying

and grunting, so the Nurse sat and patted her on and off through the night to calm her.

Her eyes are sore and she's now got conjunctivitis as well, so we've got some special cream. She is really frothy around the mouth and doesn't seem to be swallowing too well.

Corne said that Jordan will probably be left physically handicapped, although maybe not mentally as well.

We've got to try to bully Jordan out of this comatose state. I asked Debbie to tape Chloe singing and talking and to tape the kids singing at playschool, as they are her favourite things.

We've got to keep talking, reading, playing music tapes and videos. After bathing and physio, I put Jordan in the buggy and she slept fairly well.

Dr Kumar says we could be another month at least. I imagine it will be longer.

11pm - Dr Dan came in for a chat and asked me if I was happy with Jordan's treatment. I told him that I didn't think anyone could do anymore at the moment. He asked if I would prefer to go to a more local hospital, but I said no. I didn't feel that Jordan's treatment would be the same, the Nurses here know her and they know if she's having a good or bad day. I want to stay here.

I had a lovely cuddle with her today, she was even quite relaxed!

I put her in the buggy three times during the day and she slept each time. It must make a nice change of position. Even so, she vomited after having some of her drugs and went all blotchy.

Some of our previous Nurses, Beth, Bev and

Amanda, came to visit - they seemed distressed by Jordan's condition.

Thursday 5th May Day 53
This morning after changing her nappy Nurse Sally put Jordan in bed with me. It was heavenly to be able to cuddle her comfortably. She was unsure for a couple of minutes but calmed down and we both went back to sleep. It was a bit awkward with all the wires, but well worth it!

She has been in the buggy a couple of times again today. She's is generally calm and stable but I won't get too excited even though it's such a relief to see her so relaxed.

Debbie rang. She's been taping at school and is going to bring Chloe in next week - let's hope it does some good.

Jordan will be tapped and probably scanned tomorrow. She's kept her two hourly feeds down so far, so these will be increased until she can tolerate sloppy foods.

I felt tetchy this morning but calmed down, Mum was so good and while she watched Jordan I went to the market with Sally.

Jordan's operations number more than I thought:

1 tumour removal
2 external drains
1 re-entry to original site
1 reservoir
2 femoral lines
1 neckline
1 Hickman line

Poor baby. No wonder she's shut down - I would

have. I'm sure most adults would have given up by now.

Friday 6th May Day 54
I had her in bed with me again, it was lovely, I'm going to get some cuddles in. I must try to get some sleep today if she's fairly calm. We need to cool her down a bit though, her face looks a bit puffy and blotchy.

3.45pm - The Neurology Doctor says she is quite happy not to put Jordan on more medication as she's already on enough and anymore could increase the complications, plus her Dystonic movements seem to have lessened. Her seizures seem to be under control, but I don't like to tempt fate by going on about it. Her temperature seems to peak at 4am and early evening, so we'll have top keep our eyes open - apparently everyone's lowest ebb is between 3-5am.

All the Nurses seem to congregate in our room - I can go to the loo and come back to find up to five Nurses gassing away! At least Jordan has lots of company!

I've been given a bottle of glucose water to try to stimulate her lips and mouth, but there's no actual rush to drink.

A special chair has been borrowed from another ward that can be put in the cot so that Jordan can be sat up and completely supported - Corne calls it her racing chair. It is a tumble-form chair and keeps her legs apart because they now cross over like a pair of scissors.

We've got splints for Jordan's feet and ankles to wear for short periods of time to straighten out her 'in-turned' feet. They also encourage the feet to be at 90 degrees instead of pointing straight down. Her ankles are getting sore from these splints so we have got to be careful.

Now that Jordan is sitting up we can see where her bone flap has been removed, because it dips inwards.

Monday 9th May Day 57

Over the weekend Jordan seemed to be moving her left leg when asked to. She was given jam and fruit puree on a sponge. When I got back on Sunday I was so excited but then so disappointed because she was hot and spasmy. I asked for Jordan's medication to be revised more regularly and for her to get more acute care because she's so sick, especially at night. I know she's having the best care in the world, but I feel it's all got a bit complacent. I don't want things to just plod along.

I also asked for the Nurses to keep family members up to date and to explain how Jordan got into this condition, because I'm always repeating myself and I don't have any more answers.

When I think how scary that first scan was, it's nothing compared to daily occurrences now.

Corinne, a little girl patient from Malta, came in to see Jordan. She prays for Jordan and sang "Baa baa black sheep" to her. She's a lovely little girl. Lene in the next room is in a bad way. She may be paralysed down one side and who knows what else.

Nurse Lisa drew up a care plan for Jordan which is so big that it covers the bathroom door. It's so that everyone knows what time things happen or medication is given. I think Jordan may be comforted by some sort of routine. I feel rough today, am I coming down with something?

Tuesday 10th May Day 58
Jordan will have a silk nose tube inserted tomorrow which can stay in longer than the plastic ones, then an X-ray to make sure it's in the right place. I've got a cold and feel rough.

Tasha the physio tried to put Jordan in a standing frame to help prevent her leg bones becoming brittle from lack of use. The idea is to stand in it, strapped in and supported and gradually put a little weight on the legs to strengthen them.

It was a disaster! It took three of us to put her in and still that wasn't enough. Jordan was so distressed, she banged her face and we had to support her whole body. We abandoned the idea. Jordan was very shaky and she sat on Dad's lap for ages.

We tried cheesy bake baby food on a sponge, but she wasn't impressed, she was still too shaky. We'll try again tomorrow.

Jordan was stiff and restless this evening and passed some of her drugs out. She cried out a couple of times in the night, so I changed and turned her.

Jordan's nasal tube feed is separate from her TPN and is given to try to get food absorbed by her stomach, because she won't be on TPN forever.

Wednesday 11th May Day 59
I felt lousy this morning despite having Jordan in with me. Her weight is down again to 9kgs. I was hoping the nasal feed would fill her up but she vomited twice and had to have it stopped for a while.

Mum was here all day and we had smoked salmon for lunch.

I really broke down today, both on my own and with Mum. I miss Jordan so much, her kisses and cuddles, everything. I don't understand all this. Why her? It doesn't make any sense. I felt better after my sob.

We had lots of cuddles today and it felt good to get her used to being upright. We didn't try to use the standing frame today, she just had physio.

Each day goes so fast. I see the other kids running around outside. I don't feel bitter, just very sad for Jordan. She's missing so much. I just want my baby back, to love and to love me and to cuddle and to laugh with. I love her so much and would love to take it all away to give her life some quality and happiness.

Her gut is playing up, her frothing at the mouth is from reflux, which is when an amount of what goes into her stomach froths back up to her mouth. Hopefully it's not permanent.

Monday 16th May Day 64

I have started to see a counsellor in the hospital, because I'm so distressed about Jordan's condition. This is why the diary isn't up to date.

Last Friday night Jordan vomited, but it didn't come out, it went down into her lungs and she stopped breathing. A suction machine was used to clear her lungs, and she was put on anti-biotics to prevent potential pneumonia.

On Saturday we had a meeting with two of the Neurologists. Some of Jordan's brain tissue has liquified, the cells have died and turned to water. The damage is irreparable and final. This could have been caused by infection or the high pressure caused by the hydracephalus. Jordan will definitely be severely mentally and physically handicapped, that's if she survives. The Neurologists were very honest which I appreciate. My baby has been so sick and gone through so much and is so weak. Surely she can't take any more.

I've lost my Jordan and been left with another version of her. I love her just the same whatever condition she is in. I want to scream, but mostly I just cry.

They've started her nasal feed again, but we've got to keep an eye on her in case she vomits - if she catches pneumonia from fluid in her lungs it will probably kill her.

I've been thinking that Jordan will never see these diaries now, but I'll keep them going anyway, just in case, but mostly so that I remember everything. I think I've known for sometime that Jordan wasn't going to come back to me as she was before. Everyone is very cautious about what they say, but I already know. I'm her Mum and I can see what's happening.

Tuesday 17th May Day 65
Tasha did some stretching and bending with Jordan - no need for the standing frame anymore. I had to explain to some friends that the lack of anti-biotics and reduction of physio didn't mean that they had given up on her - that's one thing that they never do here.

Saw the Doctor again - nothing new. The sooner

Jordan makes some sort of recovery the better she'll be - the longer it takes the sorrier state she'll be in. Her eyesight may come back, but her uncontrolled movements will hinder other things.

My baby is never going to come back from Hell. She's locked in there and I can't stand it. If I knew she could be happy in some way I'd be happier. She'll never tell me that she loves me again, or say "Good morning sunshine" or "I not worried", "Please, mummy, silly mummy" or "Chloe's a maggit." She'll never play with my hair. She'll never watch 'Only Fools & Horses' and laugh at Del Boy, Rodney or Trigger. She'll never watch Captain Kirk in Star Trek, or Sesame Street.

My feelings are so mixed, I'm filled with excruciating pain, I have to accept what has happened and the probable final result. But I don't want to!

Wednesday 18th May Day 66
I'm in the laundry - after nine weeks I've finally got myself organised, everyone else has been doing our washing, now I can do my own.

Everyone's in a bad way, but I've only got enough for me and Jordan, I can't support anyone else.
It feels strange to be doing normal things like laundry, I feel like I am floating around. Everyone has taken our news very badly. Asking why? Surely something else can be done? Haven't they been watching and listening all this time? Maybe they didn't want to, and who can blame them? At least everyone's tried to be positive and full of hope.

I'm angry, but not with them - but I can't talk about

it. The words won't come. It''s not fair, but why keep on about it. The situation is as it is. It is not a bad dream. It's real life, very real.

Thursday 19th May Day 67
Thought we'd found a wonder drug this morning. It's side effects would have been useful for her temperature and blood pressure, but it was no good for children.

Busy day. Sally tinted my hair. I phoned Jeanette.

Friday 20th May Day68
Nurse Sally made me breakfast - Dr Kumar was jealous and I told him he just didn't have that special something! Only Jamie came today. Jordan's stable and rested well this afternoon. At about 3pm they started turning her TPN off so that she can be unhooked from the machine and I can take her for a walk in the buggy. As the liquid part of TPN can only be given for 20 hours a day we can use the time off to give Jordan a change of surroundings.

Sunday 22nd May Day 70
Had the weekend off. I miss Jordan so much, I don't suppose there'll be any improvement, just as long as she's no worse. I've got to give her lots of kisses and cuddles from everyone. Lots of phone messages, I ought to write some letters.

Monday 23rd May Day 71
Jordan is the same. We're trying a new drug for her Dystonic movements, whose side effect is an on/off effect. It's unpredictable so we'll see how it goes. She's

on a very low dose.

We've had to stop the Paracetomol because long term use can cause liver damage and we don't know if it's actually doing any good.

The occupational therapist was here working out the design of an armchair to aid Jordan's physio. When her food was finished, I took her outside in the buggy without her machines to the cafe. We went on our own - it was scary but lovely to be out with her. I don't know if she enjoyed it or not. I hadn't been outside with Jordan for ten weeks - it seems like a lifetime. I felt proud of her and talked to her constantly, explaining sounds and bumps along the path. She didn't react to anything, but seemed peaceful. I hope she wasn't afraid.

People who'd seen me on my own for so long asked how she was, what exactly was wrong and were visibly distressed although they all said how beautiful she was. I wonder what crossed their minds as they looked at her?

Hopefully we won't have to leave Parrot Ward yet. I've been told that Jordan's rehabilitation is down to the ward. I hope so. I don't want to go to another hospital, they won't know us or Jordan's ways.

She weighed 10kgs on Sunday, because her TPN is more concentrated. Kathy phoned - Sally had updated her - a very sad conversation.

I had counselling this morning. Although my counsellor is a lovely lady, I still find it hard to talk completely openly to her, I don't know why. I know it's okay if I cry with her, but it doesn't happen. It's my fault, not hers.

We're going to get Jordan's own buggy here and the

occupational therapist will check it out to see if it needs adjusting to suit her. At least it's got rain and sun shades so we can go out in most weather.

Tuesday 24th May Day 72
Jordan weighed 10.1kgs today.

Took Jordan to the gym for physio today. I had to leave. It was so distressing to see Jordan on top of a three foot high orange ball being gently bounced and rocked to relax her. She seemed to like it, but it just brought it home to me how she is going to be. She didn't look like my baby, sprawled across that ball. I ran away because I wanted to be sad on my own. Dad stayed there with her, I couldn't talk about how I felt, my heart was breaking for Jordan.

She is now taking yet more drugs, for her dystonia, her stomach lining, an anti-fungal drug and a blood pressure controller.

Wednesday 25th May Day 73
Mum took Jordan to the gym for me - I went to the launderette. Jamie's lunch hour gets longer and longer!

Sat under the trees in Queens Square with Jordan. I'm not sure but she seemed to be aware of the trees above us, her eyes were moving slowly from side to side and were wide open as if she was listening to something.

Sonia in the next room is a lovely person - even with all Lene's problems she still has time to be concerned about Jordan and me.

Dr Dan came to see us. Apparently it's been thought for some time that Jordan's temperature problem is centrally controlled, which means the brain damage she has suffered has affected that part which controls temperature. I don't know why I wasn't told before.

I feel really tired again today, must be the warm atmosphere up here.

Thursday 26th May Day 74

My Uncle Bob baptised Jordan. I'm not religious but I didn't mind, it can't do any harm. Dad treated me to lunch and dinner, I think he and the others are finally accepting that Jordan's condition is out of our hands and that we can't make her better, we can only make her as comfortable as possible, and love her more than ever.

Mum phoned as did Pat, Pauline, and Leeroy - had a good chat. Even if they can't visit I really appreciate them thinking of us and phoning.

Because Jordan is not absorbing her milk feed properly in the stomach, she is going to have a tube inserted via her nose to her jejenum, under X-ray to check it is going in correctly. She may be able to absorb the milk better then. They are looking for this to replace the TPN as a means of feeding Jordan, but I hope this doesn't mean we have to leave the ward - I feel Jordan is safest here.

Friday May 27th Day 75

I went to bed upset and woke up feeling the same. Jordan had a bad time between 8 and 12 last night, she was retching, hot and blotchy. Dad pointed out her breathing was odd so they are going to cut out her morning dose of the drug for her dystonic movements. Makes sense to me.

Jordan has gone to have her Jejunal tube inserted. I didn't go because Corne said it was not nice to watch. I feel guilty not going, but I just couldn't face it. Her Nurse will stay with her.

I had a card today from Debbie, lovely words.

When Jordan came back, I laid on her bed holding her, it was lovely. I know she's not going to open her eyes, put her arms around me and say "I love you Mummy" but I would give anything for that to happen. She seems more comfy in her own buggy, it's deeper and keeps her legs bent.

I'm so depressed today. Had counselling.

Saturday 28th May Day 76
Today I was very down and upset. I was told by a Nurse that Jordan is dying and that her odd, irregular breathing pattern is called cheyne-stoking. A couple of big breaths, a couple of smaller ones, then she stops for a couple of seconds and starts again with a big breath. It will get slower and slower and then stop altogether.

Sunday 29th May Day 77
Bad, sad atmosphere today. I found it all very distressing and difficult. I didn't want anyone to hold Jordan, I didn't want to let her go. I wanted to hang on to her forever myself.

Monday 30th May Day 78 Bank Holiday
Sharon phoned and said that one day when I was ready she would take me on holiday, she's so thoughtful.

Everyone is so very sad.

Jordan had some tapping of the fluid over the weekend. I had a row with a Doctor who wanted to tap her again today, because I had been told by someone else this was not a good idea on a daily basis, but he said "We'll have to tap until something more permanent can be found."

I asked "Like what?"

Doc said "We'll put a shunt in"

I said "She can't even have drugs because of her breathing, she'll never survive an anaesthetic, let alone surgery. She's dying, so it's not an option."

Doc "We'll withdraw treatment if that's what you want."

I said "That 's not what I said, I just want her to be comfortable."

The Doctor left the room and the charge Nurse apologised to me.

Kurt's Dad Jimmy complained that I'd been told one thing and this Doctor was now saying another. Jimmy explained that I'd accept daily tapping but not surgery, and that the Doctor shouldn't have upset me like that. Thanks Jim!

Tuesday 31st May Day 79
We all sat in the park, it was a really beautiful and sunny day.

Nobody can say how Jordan will be even at the end. There was confusion over the weekend about Jordan's feed and drugs and which tube to use. Everyone had different ideas, but I back Corne every time, because she's never let me down.

She also had a scan today. It was worse than before

- the fluid has become more dense and spread out, it's seeping into her brain and I can't see it stopping. The waterproof lining around the brain is damaged and not working for some reason, and it is not going to mend.

The Registrar was trying to be optimistic but I said "I'm her Mum and I can see what's happening to Jordan."

Sometimes I feel the situation is not real and it's all a dream, but whose imagination stretches this far? Who could make this up? After all the confusion of the last few days, it's like being dragged through hell again and again. Who knows what Jordan is going through? I hope she's too far away to know anything.

They say that her condition is very rare. There have only been a couple of cases.

This flooding of the brain is what's going to kill her.

All her senses have been switching off one by one - eating, drinking, speaking, eyesight, her bodily functions have all been going mad.

I know that the hearing is the last sense to go and then I'll know we won't have her for much longer.

Wednesday 1st June Day 80
Over the last few nights, Kurt and I have had to make decisions on resuscitation, and we decided that if Jordan stops breathing peacefully, we'll let her go with dignity. We've also made plans about final things like cremation, music etc. It's all so awful, we really didn't need to do it, but at least it's done now.

Changed my counselling until tomorrow because I wanted to take Jordan out. It was a really hot day, beautiful, so we sat in Queens Park all afternoon.

I now know that Jordan's strange breathing on Saturday was in fact because of the drugs she's on for her dystonia. Although the dose was small, twice a day proved too much. The Nurse really believed that Jordan was dying, but now the dose has been cut down she's much better. The problem is that I let everyone know the Nurses fears and now they've all been through hell. That day was appalling, Kurt was in a bad way.

Thursday 2nd June Day 81
Saw Dr Kirkam today.

Death is more likely than survival.

Jordan's condition is rare and very complicated and nobody knows what's happening, why it's happened or how to stop it. Nobody will commit themselves and I don't blame them. I said that I thought Jordan's condition would just get worse and that she would die. Nobody disagreed.

Tasha the physiotherapist was told by a Nurse that physio was no longer appropriate as Jordan's breathing was so bad, but I wasn't told this and thought Tasha had deserted us. It should have been up to Tasha. Jordan has a cold.

Friday 3rd June Day 82
Last night Jordan's cold was phlegmy and she had to have suction. We sat her up all day. An X ray showed her nasal tubes were all curled up in her stomach, so they were removed and the tube to her stomach replaced by a silk one. The jejunal tube will be replaced on Monday.

Her breathing is a bit erratic today, although she's

not so bunged up as yesterday. Her X ray showed all
the wind in her tummy, so she had to have a tube up
her bottom to release it. She'd poo'ed just before, so
most of it had moved, poor baby.

Saturday 4th June Day 83
Danuta came yesterday morning, she brought a
prayer for Jordan from her priest, and Jordan was
mentioned in the church's paper. Danuta won't be
coming again, she finds it all too distressing. I don't
blame her.

I took Jordan for a really long walk yesterday
afternoon and had a nice quiet evening all to
ourselves. She had bad wind in the night so I gave her
some gripe water. Hope it works.

Sunday 5th June Day 84
Debbie gave birth to Josh Jordan Saunders at 8.10am
yesterday, weighing in at 7lb 3oz. His middle name is
after my little angel. I think it's a wonderful thing
to do.

I've been trying to go through Jordan's stuff, there's
so much that she's never worn and never will, even if
she survives. It's not easy. I took a few bits to Debbie
for Chloe - I want them to be worn, not hidden away
or thrown out, I know Jordan wouldn't mind.

Jordan now has a urinary infection, and still has
wind, so she's on anti-biotics twice daily again.

Monday 6th June Day 85
The consultant Mr Hayward spoke to me this
morning and told me that Jordan and I can stay in our
room, thank goodness - I was dreading being told we

had to move. I think I'd have picked Jordan up, left the hospital and kept on walking. I really didn't want to move now. The thought terrifies me - if we move where people don't know us, mistakes might be made and Jordan doesn't need that now.

Mr Hayward said they'll keep treatment as gentle as possible and keep her comfy; I said I didn't want Jordan in any pain and he agreed. She hasn't poo'ed today and keeps drawing her legs up, she must be uncomfortable.

Tuesday 7th June Day 86

As well as Jordan's dystonic movements (which we have got used to) her mouth twitches very slightly as if she's trying to smile, and today she started a slight head twitch also. Just to one side and back, not very often.

Went to the park with Jordan, Sally and Alex. I am very tired today, Jordan was awake early this evening. She poo'ed a couple of times today which might help her with her wind.

We discussed Jordan's birthday today - no pressies, but we will celebrate with some food and wine etc.

We can't let the day go by unnoticed. It's still my baby's birthday.

Wednesday 8th June Day 87

Another bad night, Jordan is so uncomfortable.

The occupational therapist came this morning with some knitted round things for Jordan's hands - they are always clenched and she has to hold a wad of gauze in each hand to stop her from digging into her palms and breaking the skin. When the therapist started discussing the armchair for Jordan, I said whatever she made would just be for use in the hospital, as Jordan probably wouldn't be going home. I felt bad telling her, she looked so upset.

Yesterday I got a letter from a friend with a booklet about a woman whose child had died aged three months, having spent all that time in a neo-natal unit. It was interesting - perhaps I should write a book about all this? Jordan will never read these diaries now, so maybe I should put them to some use.

Very traumatic today. There were problems trying to insert a new jejunal tube. I think Jordan has had enough, it's so much messing about for her all the time.

Went for a walk with Jordan and Lid - got back and had a good sob for ages. Corne came in for a chat and asked me if I was worried about taking away some of Jordan's drugs, but I said "No". Why give her what she doesn't need? I was mega-depressed. Dr Kirkam feels that Jordan may slightly improve, stay the same or die.

It's no good to Jordan to stay the same as she is.

She'll have no quality of life, unable to speak or understand. No asking for kisses or cuddles, she deserves life, she had a life and should either have it again or not. To be in limbo is not good enough for her. Lid was brilliant, we had a good chat.

Still feel rotten but not as bad.

I don't know when it was, but at some point we got rid of Jordan's cot and got her a single bed. We then had both beds pushed together like a double bed, better for cuddles!

Thursday 9th June Day 88
Dad had a counselling session, I think everyone should, it helps to talk to someone outside of all this.

Friday 10th June Day 89
Depressed again.

This morning I aspirated lots of blood from Jordan's nasal tube which could have been form the trauma of having the Jejunal tube passed.

Me and Sally went for a walk with the babies - we went shopping and got nice things to eat.

Barbara and I went for a drink but there was a big fight in the pub, so we came back.

I still feel awful. Jordan is making a lot of gastric juices but not absorbing them, so they come up the nasal tube.

Last night she was awake and moving a lot until 3am, when she suddenly crashed out.

Saturday 11th June Day 90
It's two months since Jordan smiled at me. She retched badly this morning and both her tubes got pushed out. Eventually her nasal-gastric tube had to go down the other nostril. Had the night off and Kurt stayed.

Sunday 12th June Day 91
Jordan looks well - putting on weight suits her. She's very windy but I've learned how to draw the wind up through the nasal-gastric tube. It must help her.

What's the point of torturing Jordan? Her comfort is meant to be the most important thing here and I've got to insist on it because she's had enough.

Monday 13th June Day 92

Beautiful hot sunny day, not a bad night last night. Woke early to Jordan's laugh-cough sound. Got into bed with her and went back to sleep for a couple of hours. Jordan's eyelashes must be an inch long now, they're incredible. Apparently, all critically ill children grow these eyelashes. hers were lovely to start with and now they're unreal.

She's been aspirating juices all day - the noise she makes is like a sad crying and coughing sound.

We sat in Queens Park and outside the pub for a while. I dozed in the park while Dad and Albert watched over our little treasure.

We gave Jordan's bike to Sarah, the play manager on the ward, because Jordan will never ride it.

Everything is making me really angry, everyone is trying to help but I feel like I'm being invaded. Had counselling this morning.

When Jordan was born she was so perfect, gorgeous and beautiful, a wonderful baby and child. Clever and cute, nobody knew of that evil thing growing inside her head, causing damage, getting ready to ruin her life and all of our's too.

Evil, nasty awfulness.

How can there be a God? No way!!

Tuesday 14th June Day 93

Two days until Jordan's birthday. I feel very strange about it. I keep telling her that I love her. I don't know if she can hear me, but I don't care. I have to tell her. Hopefully she can feel my love when I hold her.

I'm sitting outside because it's another beautiful day. Think I've got hayfever again. My washing is in the laundry.

Took Jordan over to the park with some friends and had a little picnic. Pam and Jim watched Jordan when I went to eat, but they got distressed because Jordan went blotchy, made funny noises and her limbs started moving. It's usual early evening stuff, but it must be difficult if you don't see it everyday. She's fairly settled at the moment.

All children are precious, they shouldn't be smacked just because the parents are tired. They're not always being naughty, and the only way to learn things is to try them. It's up to us to guide them, show them right from wrong and let them live the life we gave to its fullest extent. We should encourage them to fulfil their own dreams and wishes, and expectations, without deliberately hurting anyone. To be as happy as possible, to love them unconditionally. They owe us nothing, we owe them everything.

Wednesday 15th June Day 94
Quiet day, birthday cards arriving already. I feel strange about tomorrow.

Thursday 16th June Day 95
Mum, Dad, Pam, Jim, Jamie, Joanne, Holliejade, and Kurt were here today.

My baby's third birthday. We just had the grandparents visiting. No presents, but food, wine and cake, mostly for the Nurses who've been so good.

Emma and Jerry sent Jordan and me a lovely bouquet of flowers and Barbara and Steven bought her some lovely birthday socks.

I lost my temper today. Naturally everyone was

highly strung and tense and upset, but I felt that personal feelings were in the way of what was important - Jordan. She is the only important person today, none of us matter.

I took Jordan off to the park with some wine and Sally, Alex, Jamie, Joanne and Hollie. All was well by the end of the day.

Dad gave the car he was going to buy for Jordan for her birthday to the playroom on the ward. It has a plaque on it saying "Donated by Jordan Marie Kohle-Stephens."

The Nurses bought me a bouquet of flowers and a bottle of vodka. Dad bought me a dress. A very tiring, stressful day. Today's weather was the best we've ever had on Jordan's birthday. Typical.

Maybe it's her last one?

Friday 17th June Day 96
Dr Kirkam came to say that she and Ann Goldman will both come and see me on Monday about terminal care for Jordan.

Saturday 18th June Day 97
Corne came in for a chat - Jordan has put on weight and is physically well. The TPN seems to have given her an edge. Maybe she'll have a bit more time. She's still so beautiful and gorgeous and I'm sure that inside she's as cheeky and lovable as ever.

Sunday 19th June Day 98
Had last night off. Saw Albie, Claire and baby Max who weighs 4lb now. They asked me to be his Godmother - I said yes straight away.

Monday 20th June Day 99
Jordan's dystonia is very pronounced today. I got Corne a wedding card.

Tuesday 21st June Day 100
Jordan burped tonight and passed wind a couple of times, a major achievement. Today she has been well, although a bit windy tonight. Horrible weather, only went to the cafe for lunch and came back. Jordan and I spent a lazy afternoon snoozing and watching a film snuggled up on the bed together.

Mr Hayward wants us moved, joking that I'll become institutionalised.

We could end up being moved to Dr Kirkam's ward but I don't want to go, nor do I want to go to a local hospital. After all this time, it would mean getting to know lots of new staff and they would have to get to know us.

I would rather just go home. If my honey is going to stay with me then we may as well try and get on the best we can. She looks so gorgeous at the moment, she's put on weight, her skin looks good and she's very stable.

Wednesday 22nd June Day 101
Jordan had three funny turns today, starting at 1am. We aspirated lots of blood from her stomach, it's bleeding and she looked as though she was fitting. She settled afterwards. Corne put her on drugs to line the stomach.

Another episode this afternoon. One Nurse from Neurology wasn't sure if Jordan was having a fit or a spasm, but it wasn't good. A 'jejenostomy' was mentioned, where a tube goes directly to Jordan's jejenum rather than via the nose and stomach.

Jordan's wind was like bubble wrap in her stomach, I could feel it and almost move it around. Maybe that's what's causing her movements to be worse.
Thank goodness for Emma who came and gave me a cup of tea and a cuddle. Sally came to do my roots and trim my hair.

An upsetting day, I'm very tired and distressed.

Jordan wore her new dress today that Lynn sent yesterday, it's gorgeous.

Thursday 23rd June Day 102
Jordan had a bad turn and bad wind - she needs winding like a baby and to be held upright.

Friday 24th June Day 103
Really lovely weather, lazy morning. Went for a picnic in the park with Nurse Lisa, Emma, Jerry, Barbara and Sonny. There was wine, sandwiches, cake, dips, the lot. Took photos. Lovely afternoon. Lisa brought Emma, me, Sonny and Jordan friendship bracelets.

There were storms tonight, lightning thunder and rain, it was mad.

We're being moved to Ward 1c on Monday, so I went to have a look today. I know we should move - Jordan's not really a surgical patient anymore. The Gastro people want her to have a jejenostomy so that I can take her home, if the aneasthetists agree to do it. I don't want to move anywhere else for months on end.

Saturday 25th June Day 104
Packed a load of stuff for Dad to take home for me,

because we'll have less room on the new ward. Sat outside with Jordan.

Sunday 26th June Day 105
Jordan had a good night. Kurt brought her a lovely dress yesterday.

Monday 27th June Day 106
Jordan was very unsettled all night, aspirating gastric juices every couple of hours - she must have been very uncomfortable, but luckily she settled a little this morning.

Corne had a good wedding.

Me and Jordan are moving today and Corne may be coming to work on Ward 1c - what luck!!! Jamie helped me to move and I brought a thank you card for Parrot Ward.

We've still got two single beds to make a double, so we can cuddle all night. Our new room is smaller and older, and we have to share the bath and loo facilities. Very sad at leaving Parrot Ward, we were very spoiled by them.

Dr Kumar came and said that Jordan's latest scan was no better, a little worse in fact. Her condition is obviously deteriorating.

I love her so much I could burst, she's so fragile.

Tuesday 28th June Day 107
Jordan's spasms were bad today, arching her back and staring eyes. Is it fitting?

Jordan's urine is a bit wiffy - maybe another urinary infection? Has Jordan's stabilised condition been leading up to something worse? Am I going to get my baby home?

She was very unsettled this evening, took ages to calm down - she's not been this bad for a long time.

I'm so confused and lost. What plans can we make to get her home. Or not? What's going to happen?

I want to scream and hit everyone.

Wednesday 29th June Day 108
Weather not so good today. Corne's not coming to work here after all, I'm so disappointed. Did laundry quite late.

Thursday 30th June Day 109
Last night was appalling, awake until 3.30am, then she went into a nice sleep, but later her breathing became all erratic. Extremely hot and vomiting, and we had to use suction to get it out of her throat. This happened a few times, she was shaking and very poorly, and only got a couple of hours sleep. Is her condition getting worse?

We need help, she's so bad.

I thought last night was it.

A boy in the next room called Scott has taken a shine to Jordan and comes in to speak to her. He gave her a little fluffy sticker from the hospital radio.

She could get infections all the time and it's not fair to prolong things with medication if it's her time - we want her to be pain free.

It was a bit harder actually saying it today than talking about it a few weeks ago, because now it's for real.

Jordan was unsettled this evening, and took half an hour to calm down. It was decided the new drug for pain relief had been working quite well, and she could stay with that - if it stopped working she could have morphine infusion, if she doesn't fight off the infection herself. We'll see.

Jordan has put on so much weight, she looks so well - how deceiving.

Friday 1st July Day 110
Good sleep last night but she'd poo'ed and was lying in it - so undignified for her.

Got up late, went to Sid's with Jamie and then to the park on our own. We sat in the sunshine for a while, the two of us, it was peaceful. I even took the sunshade off her buggy to get some sun on her face, just for five minutes. I talked a lot and Jordan listened.

It felt like a really special time. I couldn't stop looking at her and kissing her. How many times did I tell her that I loved her? I told Jordan that if she'd had enough and didn't want to stay that I understand. That she's been very brave and I'm very proud of her, that I'll miss her dreadfully and always love her. It's her decision and I'll go along with it. Of course, I'd like her to stay forever for me to hold and kiss, but that's selfish, especially the condition she's in now. So whatever is best for Jordan is okay by me.

We went up to Parrot Ward for a tea party. Jordan and I slept between 5 and 6.

Strange day, I feel so empty, lost and lonely. Jordan looks so lovely and peaceful. I love Jordan so much and tell her constantly. I really don't think that she can hear me now, but I'll tell her anyway. My angel is so peaceful, so gorgeous, the evil inside her head so invisible and destructive. I want what's best for her, she must be peaceful and happy, wherever she goes. I hope she'll be waiting for me when I go. I wish I could surround her with love, suck out the badness and give her a chance of life at the cost of my own.

She was so full of life and should have had the rest of it, it's not fair to stop it at three years old. Who's bright idea was it to tease her with love and life and laughter, then take it away?

Saturday 2nd July Day 111
Another bad night, as bad as Wednesday but different. Still very high heart rate, over 200, and temperature up as well. She's very uncomfortable, but she crashed from 6 to 9am after some drugs. At least it was some sleep. Her eyes are heavy and puffy and half-closed. Will they ever open again? Her breathing is not exactly laboured, but it's not good. She was breathing like a train last night, it was so loud and I woke up at 2.15am. I can't bear to see her like this.

The sooner she's out of pain the better, she's had enough over the last sixteen weeks. It's time to stop and be pain-free and peaceful. Her suffering mustn't go on.

Got put on morphine today. A canula was put in her wrist by an anaesthetist, who made me feel like he was doing me a favour. Maybe I'm not in a very sociable mood.

As it's in her wrist, she's got a splint on to keep her arm straight.

Sunday 3rd July Day 112
Corne came to see me. The truth about Jordan's last scan is that it was atrocious. Her brain has collapsed

in on itself and has lost its substance, but because the brain stem is okay, encased in the spinal column, she's still breathing. Not much else though. Tonight we got the morphine turned up. Jordan was in a bad way, she finally went to sleep from about 1am until 6am.

Jordan's deterioration has been so rapid these last few days, I'm sure it can't go on much longer.

Nurse Jacquie and I had a good chat this evening. I phoned Debbie and told her that I'm so very scared.

The pain from my fear is incredible. I hope that Jordan is not afraid and that she can't feel my anxiety.

Monday 4th July Day 113
Independence Day. It is two years since Jordan started to walk. What will she do on this Independence Day?

A lady from the pain relief team arranged things so that she can have extra morphine every 15 minutes. Whatever, Jordan must be comfortable and pain free. The morphine is now more important than her food.

I know it's all been leading up to this situation but I'm terrified.

I had let myself get mildly excited about her jejenostomy and going home. Not now though. I'm sure I won't get my baby home.

There are little burst blood vessels on Jordan's face, I think from the spasms. There's blood up her nose and lots in her stomach.

Today was my baby's last day. Decisions about medication had been made with the Doctors, who said that Jordan had pneumonia. Her breathing changed and became raspy and laboured. Her breaths got less and less, she got paler and her lips and scar lost all colour.

Jordan arrested just before 3pm for over a minute, then she came back, but her eyes never moved at all, she was completely relaxed.

As Jordan's breathing slowed down, I knew what was happening. Inside my head I was screaming "Not yet, not now, I'm not ready". But Jordan was.

Her breaths got less and less and at about 7pm they slowed right down to about four breaths every 30 seconds, and a pink bloody froth came from her nostrils. Suddenly her little body seemed to curl up, she went a blueish colour and blood came from her nose, she made a couple of little noises and then went to sleep forever.....

Nothing in this world can prepare you for death. Even if you know it's coming it's still a shock. Thank goodness Kurt and I were both there. I think she hung on for him to arrive after her arrest...so we could say goodbye together.

Dr Dan was there - I was glad because he was there at the beginning of our stay and at the end.

Everyone was lovely. We held on to Jordan for ages. I washed and dressed her in the new dress that Kurt had bought for her. The grandparents and uncles and Nurses all gave her one last cuddle. We let Jordan go around midnight.

Yesterday we registered her death:

Cause of death - pneumonia
Caused by - Encephalitis
Caused by - third ventricular astrocytoma

Good night, my angel
* * * * *

Jordan Marie Kohle-Stephens
16th June 1991-4th July 1994

An angel who brought love, joy and light
into all our lives,
Asleep now, wrapped in a blanket of love,
sweet dreams, sweetheart.

The days following the loss of Jordan are a bit hazy but interspersed with very distinct memories.

We were allowed to stay at the hospital for the night after losing Jordan. The next morning the Nurses brought tea and toast and arranged for us to visit her in the Chapel of Rest. We had a job finding it, and I was very agitated, I wanted to get to her. When we arrived we were shown in to a beautiful chapel. I remember the flowers and high table covered in fabric, with a pillow and my beautiful baby laying on top in her lovely dress and frilly socks. She looked so peaceful and lovely. I kissed her and stroked her arm and rearranged the little blanket that partially covered her, as if she would get cold. Of course I cried, the whole situation didn't seem real. We stayed for a while just crying and looking at her - but I knew she was gone, she wasn't going to open her eyes and ask for a cuddle.

A couple of Nurses had waited outside for us and they visited Jordan to say goodbye. That afternoon we had to register Jordan's death - it seemed a cold and unkind thing to do. The registrar was sympathetic without being patronising, but it felt like we were signing end of lease papers.

After seeing the registrar we collected mine and Jordan's things from the hospital, said goodbye to the staff and left.

At some point, we had asked Jamie to phone round

some funeral parlours for us. He found one nearby and went to speak to a lovely lady named Moira. She said she would send for Jordan straight away and that she'd call as soon as she arrived so that we could visit her.

The Co-Op funeral parlour was marvellous. They didn't charge for children's funerals and you only had to pay if you wanted extra cars. Looking back, this was a very generous thing to do, grieving parents don't need extra worries about trying to find money.

Moira called the next day and I went straight to the funeral parlour. She left me alone in the Chapel Of Rest. She'd arranged some flowers in there and I sat next to Jordan's little white coffin and talked to her. I told her lots of things, how much I loved her and missed her, but that I was glad she was now free from pain. I said I hoped she was having a lovely time wherever she was.

Although I believed that Jordan's spirit had left her body and I didn't need to visit the parlour to talk to her, I still wanted to look at her and touch her until the time came when I couldn't anymore. It comforted me that each day I could kiss her and say "See you tomorrow."

The weekend came and, although I'm sure Moira would have opened up especially for me to visit Jordan, I didn't ask her. However, when I arrived on the Monday I was shocked at how discoloured Jordan was. I knew it would happen, but it was still distressing. Even so, I was glad that Moira hadn't tried to cover Jordan's face with make-up - she was only three after all.

On the day of Jordan's cremation, Wednesday 13th

July, I went to see her one more time. I put a letter each from me and Kurt into her coffin, as well as a Mr. Blobby, Sammy the Seal and a couple of small toys.

I had three creamy white roses, one for each of Jordan's innocent years, tied with ribbon for the top of her coffin. Kurt and I held one each and the rest I put inside with Jordan and her toys.

We'd asked people to donate money to the Parrot Ward at G.O.S.H instead of flowers, but left it to everyone to do whichever they preferred. Most people did both. The flowers began to arrive early in the morning, lots and lots of beautiful arrangements with thoughtfully worded cards. One that sticks out in my mind was a large teddy bear made from yellow flowers. A nice sum was also raised for G.O.S.H.

The Reverend had been to visit Kurt and I to talk about Jordan and to look at photos of her, and he gave a lovely service.

I had written some words of thanks that I wanted him to read out for me. My Dad had too and wanted to read them himself, but I couldn't bear to watch him read those special words and try to be brave in front of everyone, so the Reverend did that for us as well.

The two grandads carried Jordan's tiny coffin into the Chapel. The music we chose for the beginning and end of the service was Prince's 'The Most Beautiful Girl In The World'. We felt it was almost written for her. The crematorium was packed solid, it was hard to believe that a three year old had touched the hearts of so many people, and I felt proud when the Reverend said as much during the service.

As Jordan's coffin went behind the curtains, I wanted to run over and grab her out of there and run away to hold her forever and never let go - but I didn't. Everyone went outside to look at all the lovely flowers that people had sent. It was a blur, lots of people hugging and crying and saying hello. We all went to a local hall provided by my friend Jo's parents to eat and drink. Another friend's Mum, Joyce, provided the food. Everyone gave their time and didn't charge us - we didn't have to think of anything, and for that I will always be grateful. Later on, we went with a couple of friends for a meal but by now 'automatic pilot' had really set in and I don't remember much of what was said. I do know that everyone was thoughtful and kind that day.

Many things helped me cope during Jordan's ordeal. The support from everyone was obviously vital, but I also gained strength from the counselling, involving myself in every stage of her illness, allowing myself to cry and of course, my diary.

Keeping the diary was obviously of great help. But also, learning as much as I could about everything that was going on with Jordan was vital. Everytime something about Jordan's condition changed, I would ask questions so that I understood what was going on as much as possible. The medical staff were often baffled because her condition was so rare, but they tried everything and did their best for her, and to keep us up to date on her complications. This helped me a lot, knowing as fully as possible what we were dealing with. I was even allowed to borrow the staff medical books to read up on Jordan's different medical conditions.

While in hospital I also felt it was important for me to do as much as possible for Jordan. I couldn't leave normal everyday things like washing and dressing her for the Nurses to do. I even did some physiotherapy that Tasha showed me each day as well as her regular sessions. I would also massage Jordan with cream or diluted Tangerine oil to relax her stiff limbs. This had the added effect of being another form of close physical contact, which I made sure she got lots of.

As Jordan's Mum, I felt that if I talked to her all the time, read to her, played her videos, kissed, cuddled and massaged her, it might comfort her. After Jordan lost all her communication skills, I thought that all these things would be reassuring, that somehow somewhere inside she would know it was me doing these things. I told her constantly that I loved her just in case she understood.

I am so glad now that Jordan and I slept together in hospital. I could hold her as much as possible - I hoped it would be good for Jordan, it certainly was for me. Plus, this also ensured that I was immediately aware during the night if anything was wrong. I used to love just watching Jordan when she was having a lovely peaceful sleep, when her body was still and her breathing regular. She was so beautiful throughout her illness. I used to wish that her poor little body could always be relaxed.

One of the Mums in the hospital told me that she'd passed our room one morning, and looking in had seen Jordan and I asleep together with the sun shining through the window on to us. She said it was a beautiful sight that she would always remember. I think the lady's name was Sarah. I try to picture what she saw that day and it gives me a lovely memory, the two of us sleeping peacefully together, bathing in sunlight.

People wanted to make sure that I ate properly whilst in hospital, and I did. I knew I had to keep my strength up to be able to do my best for Jordan, so I appreciated all the special things they brought in for me.

Despite being hard on them sometimes, my friends

and family were always so supportive. They did all the practical things, like washing our clothes whilst we were in the hospital, bringing in food and helping financially, all the things that are so difficult to do when you're not in your own home for any length of time.

People phoned and visited from far and wide because they were concerned that we didn't feel lonely. Situations like ours make you feel isolated, but the tremendous support we had helped to carry us through. I appreciated *every* phone call, especially people who phoned just to say "I'm here if you need me" or "I'm thinking of Jordan everyday."

The counselling I had also helped because with everything being so intense I found it easier to talk to a non-family member about everything. When taking to those who were suffering as intensely as I was, I would feel their pain and I just couldn't cope with more than my own and how I felt about Jordan's suffering. As a result I was probably quite hard on those closest to me. At no point in hospital did I dare allow myself into a situation where I would 'let go'. I felt that if I allowed that to happen I would never regain the strength I needed to look after Jordan.

I also thought that if Jordan could feel any strength from me it would help in her struggle. She was so brave and didn't complain that I just had to hold it together for her sake.

When I was alone with Jordan I did cry sometimes, and I always apologised to her for being weak. I was desperate for her not to be surrounded by a depressing atmosphere, but sometimes when I held her and spoke to her or sang her one of the songs we used to sing together and she couldn't join in, it all got too much.

I remember one morning standing looking out of the window, holding Jordan's stiff little body against mine, her hand gripping my T-shirt and her head nestled into my neck. Her Hickman line trailed from her body to her bags of liquids and food. I was rambling on, telling her that she could go down the slide outside when she was better and that I couldn't wait for when she could smile at me again and spread her arms wide and say "I love you this much." As I talked I knew it would never happen, that all the love in the world wouldn't fix what was wrong with my baby. I felt so helpless being unable to make her better. After all, that's what Mum's are for, to make things better and to take away the pain. At that moment, if someone had opened a door and said to me "Come this way both of you, Jordan will get better but there's no going back" I'd have gone. But no-one did. So I cried instead, I cried and cried. Mrs James, the play-nurse, came into our room and hugged us both. Although I didn't like to cry, it was a wonderful release of tension, and still is. I always feel stronger afterwards.

It is important to do whatever you need to do to cope with a difficult situation. If you need to scream and cry, do it. If you need to talk , do it. If you need to write down your feelings, do it. Whatever it is that will keep you strong enough to keep going can't be wrong. Only you will know what's best for you and your child.

Whatever you do, never give up.

coping after

At first waking up without Jordan was intolerable. Just getting out of bed each day was a major achievement for me and I welcomed each night hoping I wouldn't wake up the next morning.

Everyday situations were so tiring and difficult. Sometimes when the phone rang I just wanted to scream. Chit-chat was so difficult, but I was aware that people were trying very hard to be supportive. So I didn't scream and instead tried to hold 'normal' conversations, although I felt anything but normal.

Gradually my sleeping patterns became more settled. I would go for weeks not being able to sleep enough, then I would be okay for a time and then I would change back again. I never resorted to anti-depressants or sleeping tablets because I was afraid I wouldn't be able to stop taking them. If I can't sleep now I take herbal sleeping tablets.

Keeping my diary was just good therapy not just in hospital, but also since then. As I wrote the diary, it helped to put each day into some sort of perspective, to help me grasp more of the situation and write down my feelings as they came, so they were clearer when remembered. When I first read through those four months it was painful beyond belief, but it did put things in order in my mind. Otherwise it would have been impossible to remember everything exactly as and when it happened. When I read it, it's still painful and I can take myself back to that day or situation, and feel how I felt then. At the same time, it helps to release my feelings, which must be better for me than suppressing them.

It is *not* a form of self-torture however - I can never forget, so I'd rather remember properly.

I had started Jordan's diary when she was about seven months old, so it's good for me to look back and remember the happy memories, the nice things, like her first tooth, her first word, her first steps. The bad memories used to be foremost in my mind, but now it's easier for the good ones to replace them.

Her photographs bring me great pleasure. When Jordan was well I used to joke that she must be the most photographed and video-ed child ever. Now of course, I'm so glad. I don't have to struggle to remember events, I look at her photos and my memory gets jogged about so many things.

When some people lose a close relative, they put away all their belongings and photographs of that person. To me, that would be shutting Jordan away. Even if I tried I don't think I could manage that. She's on my mind as soon as I wake up and I always say "Good morning" to her. I remember one day before her hospital stay when we woke up and the sun was pouring through the bedroom window and Jordan said "Good morning sunshine." I loved the way she said it! It was lovely, and on sunny days I can still hear her little voice saying it.

So, I have Jordan's photos all around me, I smile at her and talk to her and feel she's near me.

Jordan's toys and clothes were all packed away for a time. I gave a few toys away to special people and friends' children. Some of her clothes I gave to Chloe, Jordan's best friend. She liked wearing them but now she's outgrown them I've put them away again.

There are some things that I couldn't give to anyone. Maybe in time I will, maybe not. I only give things to those who understand how precious they are. I get pleasure from seeing her toys played with, because they are being enjoyed as Jordan enjoyed them.

I still cry at certain programmes on TV that Jordan enjoyed so much, but I don't avoid watching them because I can also laugh at the funny things she used to say and do. I can sing along to songs she liked and imagine her little voice singing with me.

And so life after Jordan began. It was after a chat with Rosina, who said to me "You have two choices - to carry on or not", that I knew if I was to carry on, I would have to do it the best way I could. I didn't want to feel that Jordan would be ashamed of me.

One of the loveliest things that anyone did for me was when my friend Sharon took me away on holiday. Initially it was for one week but we ended up staying for a month. She wanted to give me space to think, to rest and to get some sunshine.

Although all my family were marvellous, I needed time on my own to get my mind in some sort of order, to sort out my thoughts and to slow down. I had been mentally and physically on overdrive for a long time and I was exhausted. On the holiday I slept well, ate well and relaxed. We went out most nights, but I knew if I wanted to return to our room at any time, then Sharon would take me back. I was more able to cope with mixing with people if I had this escape route - I still feel like this sometimes, but not to the same extent.

Sharon has some friends at the holiday resort, they knew my situation and were very good to me. Until they got to know me, they didn't ask questions, but just let me be myself. I made some good friends that summer and we're still in touch.

Someone put it to me that I was "running away from things" by going away. But you can't run away from pain or memories, and the change of scenery and company was refreshing and gave me more strength to carry on.

Yes, I did enjoy myself - it's *okay* to laugh or cry whatever your situation.

Many things became clear to me while I was away - one was to take nothing for granted, anything can happen to change a situation at any time, it's okay to plan ahead but be flexible, be ready for change.

Another thing is that if you have a family, things like housework and gardening are not important, children come first, spending time with them is paramount, and for anyone at all life should be lived to the full, opportunities should be grabbed as they come along , there's not always a second chance.

Material possessions don't mean much at all anymore. My family and friends are the most important, and life is too short to bear grudges, or to carry negative feelings around.

I still see Chloe, and her parents Debbie and Stewart. Chloe still mentions Jordan and asks questions about her, which are not always easy to answer, but her parents and I try to be as honest as possible. Jordan's cousin Hollie is the same. They were both too young to understand the situation properly, but old enough to realise that Jordan wasn't around anymore, so we didn't make up any elaborate stories about where she was. They had both been to see Jordan in hospital and understood that she was poorly, so we just told them that Jordan had gone to a special place because she was too poorly to stay with us, and that we couldn't visit her, but that she was okay. This satisfied them for a while. They might ask more questions as they get older, who knows.

After losing their own child, some people can't face any other children for a long time, it is too painful. Fortunately, I only had a problem with large groups of children, because I wanted to see Jordan running and playing as they were.

I couldn't turn away from other children because none of them reminded me of Jordan, apart from Hollie's little sister Devon, who bears some resemblance. My brother and his wife Lisa had a son last year, he was born two days after the first anniversary of Jordan's death. I was pleased for them that Nyal didn't arrive on July 4th. I can't not enjoy my friends and family's children - they wouldn't understand if I suddenly shunned them, they're all too precious.

I met many, many parents of sick children at the Hospital and we all coped very differently with our situations, because each one was unique.

Some parents found comfort and strength in their faith or religion to carry them through their particular situation. Others became disillusioned or turned away from their previous beliefs asking themselves "Why, if there's a God, is he doing this my child?"

Those who turned to religion for help or guidance only wanted the best for their child and were doing their utmost to gain strength and be as positive as possible in the hope that it would help their child.

I myself am not religious. I wasn't before and didn't feel the need to turn to religion. Some of my family and friends are, and a lot of prayers were said for Jordan. Some even had special services at their own church. I looked on all these prayers by caring people as positive thought, and there's nothing wrong with that.

Only one person tried to convert me but soon gave up. We are all free to believe in what is best for us, whatever gives us the most comfort or strength.

Personally, I believe that there is a better place to go when our time is up here, a place where the physical pain and suffering of life disappear and peace is found. We all suffer to varying degrees throughout life, so there must be something good at the end of it all. I have always found it comforting to feel that spirits of friends and family are around me at times, although we always miss the physical presence of the people that have passed away. I like to think that they are in a better place, hopefully with friends or family that they had lost.

Consequently, I have always believed in the gift of genuine clairvoyancy, but had never been to one until after I had lost Jordan.

At first I was having dreadful nightmares and panic attacks. So I went with my Dad to the Spiritualist

Association in London and saw a lady named Margaret. She told me things about myself and then said "You have a child in the spirit world, dear."

Although contact with Jordan was what I had wanted, her words made me jump and I was very shaken. She carried on to describe Jordan to me, including her illness and the struggle in the hospital. She told me that family were looking after Jordan, that her pain and suffering were gone, and that she was 100% well and running and playing like any normal three year old. Although I would have preferred her to be doing those things here with me, I knew that couldn't be so I was elated for Jordan. I was happy that she was happy and not alone or afraid. Jordan used to say to me "I not worried mummy" and after my first visit I could almost hear her say it.

The relief was enormous. Margaret assured me that Jordan was never far away from me - this comforted me and stopped my nightmares and panic attacks. So now I visit a clairvoyant every few months for reassurance that Jordan is well. I am always satisfied, because I am told personal things that can't possibly be made up. My belief has been a great comfort to me - as long as Jordan is okay, then I'm content.

My greatest fear has always been that she would be afraid at some time and I wouldn't be there to help her. But she has nothing to be afraid of now.

Through all of my thinking and reflections on what I have learned about life and people, I realised that I had to accept what had happened to Jordan, that there's no point in continually asking "why did it happen to her?" I can't carry on by asking questions that don't have answers, it would drive me mad.

My acceptance of the situation has kept me going. Part of that acceptance is that while I was away on holiday with Sharon, I realised I was a fatalist. What will be will be, there's a reason for everything even if we never discover what that is. We should learn something positive from every situation, whether that be not to repeat your mistakes or to strive to do something better next time.

To carry on living I had to accept the situation, and to do the best I can in my life without Jordan. It's not always easy, but I didn't choose the easy option.

I have to be positive or Jordan's suffering will have been in vain, and that I can't accept.

My emotions have been very mixed - there are no rules or regulations. I have despaired, not wanting anyone to get close to me but that has often been mixed with wanting to be cuddled and to be able to cry freely. Mostly I have cried alone. When I do this, I explain to Jordan that it's because I miss her and I'm sorry she had to suffer so badly. At the same time, I'm glad that she's gone to another place where she's no longer suffering and is free to run and play and have fun.

Grief takes many forms and everyone grieves in their own way and must do whatever is right for them at the time. Some people become very angry and bitter against the world and everyone in it.

Others turn inwards, not communicating well, becoming almost childlike and needing to be looked after. For various reasons, I find it easier now to discuss my feelings, to say when I'm having a bad day or a good day.

For myself, I can say I've been angry on and off. The thing that has made me most angry is other people telling me what is best for me, what I should do next, how I should plan my future. I still find it difficult to plan too far ahead, but I don't really need to.

My closest friends and family have let me be myself, let me keep my pain to myself, because I didn't want to share it. Jordan was my daughter, I gave birth to her, no-one knows how I feel and I wouldn't wish it on anyone.

Above all else, I am still here. I still laugh and I still cry. I will always miss Jordan.

afterword

Jordan left this world as she came into it, innocent and beautiful inside and out. She knew only kindness and love from those around her. We didn't have her for long, but she made a mark on everyone's lives who knew her.

I'm proud that for whatever reason I was chosen to be Jordan's Mum, it was an honour to love and be loved by her. I've got so many lovely memories of our time together and when I'm low they help me through.

I've got a long time to wait for the next kiss and cuddle from Jordan, but I know it will be worth waiting for.